The
Emma Campbell Groves
Literary Collection

Breadsticks and Blessing Places

Breadsticks and Blessing Places

Candy Dawson Boyd

Macmillan Publishing Company
New York

For Robert Julian Boyd

Macmillan Publishing Company
866 Third Avenue, New York, N.Y. 10022
Collier Macmillan Canada, Inc.

Printed in the United States of America

10 9 8 7 6 5 4 3 2 1

Library of Congress Cataloging in Publication Data

Boyd, Candy Dawson.
   Breadsticks and blessing places.

   Summary: A twelve-year-old black girl's preparations for the King Academy entrance exam are disrupted when her best friend is killed.
   1. Children's stories, American. [1. Death—Fiction. 2. Schools—Fiction. 3. Afro-Americans—Fiction] I. Title.
PZ7.B69157Br   1985   [Fic]   84-43021
ISBN 0-02-709290-9

Contents

Breadsticks and Blessing Places

1

One Plus One Is Three

Why didn't I study for the test? Toni shifted in her seat. Raymond, her friend since kindergarten, smiled at her, but she felt too miserable to smile back.

Toni looked up into her teacher's dour face. "Antoinette Douglas, see me before you go to lunch," he ordered as he handed Toni her math test.

"Yes, Mr. Ashby." Toni ignored the curious stares of her sixth-grade classmates.

"Don't worry, Toni, we can study this weekend," said Mattie, her girlfriend, leaning over from the next seat to look at Toni's test. "Oh, no!"

Raymond looked, too. "That's bad," he said.

"A thirty." Toni moaned. "I'll never get into King Academy with these scores."

Mattie's thin face creased with a mixture of concern

3

and anger. She bit her lip. "I told you to study," she whispered, "but instead you wasted your time writing Susan letters that she doesn't even bother to answer!"

"Thanks a lot for your sympathy! I don't need you giving me a hard time," said Toni, shoving the test papers deep into her desk. "Go on to lunch. Don't bother to wait for me."

Then Toni's anger turned into a lump of pure misery as she stood beside Mr. Ashby's cluttered desk, watching him yank his fingers through the gray, wiry hair that exploded from his head. Everything on him was rippling. First his eyebrows jumped. Then his eyes blinked several times, his nose twitched, and his mouth jerked up and down at the corners.

"Antoinette, how do you expect to pass the entrance exam for King Academy at the end of March? Do you realize that's only six months away? Six months, Miss Douglas," he repeated, removing his thick glasses and rubbing his eyes.

Suddenly Toni knew how Carl, her seven-year-old brother, felt the time he came home with a bad grade in conduct.

"I'll try harder, Mr. Ashby," she said, her usually confident voice low and subdued. "I just can't get word problems."

"You rush through your work and make careless mistakes. And, Toni," he said, "don't you realize the math test on the entrance exam will include fractions? Between word problems and fractions, you won't score high. I don't understand. I've worked so hard to help you."

Toni's freckled face began to ripple like Mr. Ashby's. Fat tears filled her brown eyes and spilled out, clouding the blue glasses she hated.

"It's not you, Mr. Ashby. You're a good teacher. Sometimes I understand, and then I get more confused than ever," Toni said. "My parents will really be mad at me for getting a thirty."

"I want every problem corrected and handed in tomorrow," he told her. "And have your parents sign this test. Understand?"

Toni wished she were dead. "Yes, Mr. Ashby."

Mattie was waiting outside the classroom door, humming to herself. Her small frame rested against the cream-colored walls.

"Well, how bad was it, on a scale of one to ten?" she asked.

"How about one hundred?" mumbled Toni. "What did you get on the test?"

"Ninety-eight."

Silently they headed for the lunchroom. Toni grabbed a lunch tray and some food and strode to the table on the far left, where she, Mattie, and Susan always ate. Mattie trailed behind. The lunchroom was unusually noisy for a Monday, but Toni welcomed the din.

"Look, Toni, I'm sorry you got a thirty. Do you want to study with me this weekend?" Mattie said, taking out her favorite sandwich—mustard, sharp cheddar cheese, and two slices of tomato on wheat bread.

Toni frowned. Mattie meant just her, not Susan. She and Mattie Benson had been best friends since second grade. Then Susan Lawrence had transferred to Walker Elementary School two years ago.

"Can Susan come, too, if she's back?" Toni asked.

"No."

"Come on. She's been gone two weeks and she's going to be behind in math, too. She'll work hard," Toni said, talking with her mouth full of fries. "I promise, Mattie."

"Toni, I'm going to get into King Academy to study voice! I can't afford to waste my time with Susan," Mattie said.

"Susan's always nice to you. Why don't you like her?"

"Do you want to study with me or not?"

"Okay, I'd better," said Toni. The reluctance on her face was obvious, but she didn't care. Mattie was being unfair!

The afternoon in Room 308 sped by. Toni sat in the lowest math group, erasing and scribbling, struggling to solve the word problems.

At the end of the day, loaded down with textbooks, notebooks, and library books, Toni and Mattie ambled over to the primary kids' exit to pick up Carl. Toni turned to see if Raymond was behind them. He wasn't.

Lately he hadn't been around after school. Toni wondered where he was, but she knew she didn't need to worry about Raymond.

"Toni! Toni! I got a star on my picture!" Carl yelled, deserting his friends, Jon Ella and Harry Edwards, to run to her.

Thrusting the torn, grubby paper into her hands, he ran about in circles, yelling, "Zoom! . . . Zoom! . . . Zoom!" With his gray eyes, curly cinnamon hair, and glasses, Carl looked like a baby owl—a baby owl in a red jacket.

"Can Jon Ella and Harry Edwards come over for juice and cookies?" he roared in the middle of a turn. The cousins stood waiting, like two small sentries.

"You know Mama won't let you have company now that she's working full time," Toni reminded him.

"But you get to have Mattie and Susie over. I want my friends to come," he said, planting himself squarely before her.

"Carl, don't mess with me today. You fight that out with Daddy and Mama. Now come on!" Toni said, walking on with Mattie.

After saying good-bye to his friends, Carl caught up with them. "Where's Susie?" he asked, reaching into his pocket for a lemon drop covered with lint. "Is she sick?"

"I told you she's fine, Carl. Her father sent for her. She's still in New York City visiting him," Toni said.

"Oh." Carl started singing a song to himself. When

the light turned green, he took his sister's free hand and pulled her across the street. Mattie took his other hand.

"Why does her father take Susie away?" he asked.

"Because he wants to see her," Mattie said.

"Mattie, you want to come over for a while? We can study."

"I can't now. I have to baby-sit for the Bacons this afternoon. I'll call you later, and we can work over the phone. I'd better hurry. Bye. Bye, Carl," Mattie said, dashing down another street. Her short, dark hair was covered with a tam that threatened to tumble off.

The October sky hung over the South Side of Chicago like a periwinkle flower surrounded by bits of fluffy white baby's breath. The air was cool but not chilly. It was heavy-sweater or jacket weather. Toni breathed deeply and wished for July and long, lazy days with no math problems or tough tests to worry about.

Carl skipped and hopped along. Their journey home took them past the mailbox on the corner; past Samuel's boarded store front; past Wilson's dry cleaners, with bars on the door and the windows; past Mr. Randolph's grocery store, with bars everywhere, and Mr. Harrison, the part-time security guard; past the abandoned buildings and trashy vacant lots.

As they went up the steps to the large, brick building they lived in, Carl let loose a yelp and rushed to the door. Mrs. Elvira Stamps and her German shepherd, Hannibal, were just coming out.

"Now, this is the kind of October that makes me long for Paris, a stroll down the Avenue des Champs-Élysées, followed by a glass of dry champagne in a sidewalk cafe!" said Mrs. Stamps, her eyes twinkling behind red glasses trimmed in gold. "How are you, Carl darling and Toni my dear?"

Toni smiled. The way Mrs. Stamps caroled "Carl darling and Toni my dear" made the words one fluid musical note.

"Not so good. I failed the math test," she said.

"Dear me, and that big test is coming up in the spring, isn't it? Carl, are you coming down to visit me this afternoon? I made some carrot cake for you."

"Yes, yes, yes!" He planted a juicy kiss on her wrinkled cheek.

Toni giggled softly. Carl hated carrots. All he had heard Mrs. Stamps offer was cake. Wait until he discovered what the orange things in the cake were. He'd spit it out!

"And Toni? You are invited, too."

"If I can finish all of this homework. But I'll send Carl down," she promised.

"Excellent. This is day three of my new health and fitness regime. I plan to walk two miles today, with Hannibal as my protector." And, with that, she waved good-bye jauntily.

Toni pulled out a thick strand of orange yarn that hung around her neck and inserted the mailbox key. Carl ran ahead.

I don't believe it. Nothing! I wrote three letters, and

she hasn't even sent a postcard! Toni rechecked the mail to make sure there was nothing from Susan.

The three-floor climb to their apartment was quiet. As soon as Toni opened the two locks on the door, Carl threw himself inside and headed for the kitchen. Toni dropped her books in the living room and searched for a note from her mother on the telephone table. There it was.

While reading the note, she took off her jacket and walked down the hall past Carl's bedroom. She peeked in. It was a mess. Toni stepped in to assess the work she had to make Carl do. Just inside the doorway, she tripped and fell, landing on her left side. The culprit, a silver and black toy racing car, tumbled over, its wheels spinning in the air.

"Darn it, Carl Andrew Douglas, you get your little butt in here!" Toni screamed. Gingerly she ran her hands up and down her left leg and foot. Slowly she straightened, testing her weight on that leg. "Carl, you heard me! Get in here!"

Holding a cracker in one hand and a glass of grape juice in the other, Carl perched outside the room.

"You see this? This is your toy! Where do your toys belong? Not in the doorway for me to fall over. In your toy box. Or on your bed. Or under your bed. Do you hear me?"

"I'm sorry, Toni," he said, munching on the cracker. As soon as she turned away, he drifted down the hall toward the living room and the color television.

"Carl, don't you dare turn on that TV. Mama told you no TV until she gets home," she said to the empty doorway.

Toni listened. She couldn't hear the TV. That didn't mean anything. Carl enjoyed sitting six inches from the television with the sound turned way down. Right now it wasn't worth the trip to check on him.

Limping a little, Toni reread her mother's instructions. Carl's bedroom had to be straightened, the salad had to be made, the table set, the garbage taken out, the hamburger divided into four patties, and the potatoes peeled. And the P.S. said to watch Carl, feed Carl, do her homework.

"Not much," Toni murmured ruefully. "By the time I do all this, Mama should be home. Then Daddy will come, and the trouble will start."

In her own room, she changed from her corduroy slacks and western-style blouse to a pair of comfortable jeans and top. As she pulled the sweatshirt over her undershirt, Toni grimaced, feeling the tenderness in her small, developing breasts. They hurt when she touched them and when fabric rubbed against them.

She went into the bathroom and locked the door. She sprinkled talcum powder on her hand. Carefully Toni patted the powder on each breast. Then she positioned a soft tissue over each one, using her old, too-tight undershirt to keep them in place.

What's the matter with my breasts? Toni wondered. *Why do they hurt? Maybe I have some kind of disease.*

I'd better ask Susan when she gets back. She'll know.

Two hours later, Toni had completed most of her tasks and sent Carl to visit with Mrs. Stamps when the phone rang.

"Yes, the Douglas residence."

"Hi! We can get a problem or two done now. I'm home and Matt's at basketball practice—as usual," Mattie said. "And Mom's taking a nap."

"Oh, okay."

"You don't have to sound so disappointed. I know you want Susan to call you, not me."

"That's not true, Mattie," Toni said. "I just finished Mama's list. I'll get my books and a pencil. Hold on one minute."

Toni ran to the living room and grabbed the math book, a notebook, her black pencil case, and the test. Sighing, she reached for the receiver and settled in for a session with Mattie.

The two friends worked without a break for the next forty minutes. "I've got to stop and fix dinner before Mom gets up. Why don't you call me later, and we'll correct some more."

"Okay. Thanks a lot, Mattie." Relieved, Toni hung up and stretched. Study sessions with Mattie were exhausting. She never gave Toni the answer, not even a clue. Mattie just kept at her until she figured out the steps or gave up.

At about that time, Toni heard her mother and Carl come in. Mrs. Douglas was a compact woman, as neat and orderly as a carton of eggs.

"I don't believe it, Toni! Do you know that Gloria had the nerve to announce that she is pregnant, *again,* and that her husband wants her to stay home! For a whole year! That leaves me to handle all of the physics department and Professor Molinardi's constant demands! They don't pay me enough to put up with this mess!" She pulled her coat onto a hanger and slammed the hall closet door. "I tell you, working at the university is no picnic!"

"Hi, Mama," Toni said. "I did everything you had on the list, and I'm finishing my homework."

"Good girl." Her mother's slate gray eyes rested on her. "I'm going to get out of this suit and into something that moves with me, not against me. Carl, you turn off that television set right now. I want to see a book in your hand." Mrs. Douglas headed for her bedroom, and Toni waited for her at the kitchen table.

Following their daily routine, Toni and Mrs. Douglas worked side by side in the large kitchen. Toni noticed the empty grape-juice container on the counter, so she took a can of frozen concentrate out of the freezer.

"Gloria has four children already. Your father and I can barely afford the two of you, and God help me if we had any more! How was school today?" She changed subjects abruptly, throwing Toni off guard.

Toni's eyes dropped. The juice swirled like a churning, purple mountain stream. "Okay."

"Okay is not enough. I want some sentences strung together to answer questions like did you get the math test back? How did you do? Did you understand what Mr. Ashby taught you today?" Mrs. Douglas leaned against the sink, holding a potato masher.

"Yes, Mama, I got the test back and I understood part of the work."

"And?" Her mother moved to the table and pulled out two chairs.

"I didn't do so good," muttered Toni.

"And exactly what does 'didn't do so good' mean, daughter?" asked her father, Harold Douglas, appearing in the kitchen doorway. Carl was at his side.

"Honey, you're home early. Carl, let your father get his coat off," Mrs. Douglas said, rising to kiss her husband.

"Hi, Dot. Carl, give me a hug. I got through with the Proctor account faster than I thought I would," he said, not taking his eyes off his daughter. He was a tall, serious man, balding and fit.

"Hi, Daddy." Toni kissed him, too.

"Enough, Carl. I want to talk to your sister. Go play in your room. Toni, what was your score? Where's the test?" he asked, opening the refrigerator door and taking out a beer.

"In my room. I got a thirty," she said in one scared breath.

"A thirty won't get you into King. What did Ashby say?" Mr. Douglas asked, sinking wearily into a chair at the table.

"That I have to work hard. That I can do it."

"Then that's what you're going to do. We want you

to go to King Academy. It's one of the best college-prep public schools in Chicago."

Toni sighed.

"Toni, you do everything else so well. I know you can learn this," Mrs. Douglas said.

Toni felt that she was being pressed from every side. Nobody listened to her! They just talked and talked and talked. They all expected too much from her, and *they* included her parents, Carl, Mattie, Mr. Ashby, and even Susan.

Toni simply nodded at her parents and excused herself. Then she jumped up and ran to the bathroom, locking the door behind her.

It just isn't fair! Nobody asks me if I want to go to King! I'm over twelve years old, almost a teenager. No baby. But they treat me like I'm five. Do this! Do that! Well, I'm not going to! she vowed, sitting on the edge of the bathtub. *I'm not going to!*

"I have to go! Hurry! Open the door."

Toni dabbed at her eyes and unlocked the bathroom door. Holding his hand between his legs, Carl hopped from one foot to the other.

"Don't look," he said, quickly raising the toilet seat.

She complied, turning to face the bathrobes hanging from the wooden hook on the door. As she did, she caught her reflection in the mirror. Her brown face was highlighted by a chain of dark freckles that trailed across her upper cheeks and over the bridge of her nose. A few dotted her forehead, chin, and jaw. Large, intelligent eyes stared back at her. The plump body that had been her birthright was going through a meta-morphosis. *Not like Susan.* She frowned. *Susan looks like a model.* But a distinct waistline was emerging. She felt and looked leaner. Hooking her fingers in the space between her jeans and waist, she was stunned to see so much room.

"You can turn around now," Carl said. "What were you crying about?" He flushed the toilet.

"None of your business."

"Yes, it is," he said as he plopped down on the edge of the bathtub.

"Carl, go back to whatever you were doing and leave me alone."

"No, I won't. When I cry, you make me tell you what's wrong," he reminded her. He rummaged in his pants pocket for lemon drops. "Here, I can have one and you can have one and that makes two."

"Why doesn't one plus one equal two for me?" said Toni, leaning against the door.

One letter written to Susan should equal one letter from Susan. One smart girl in reading and writing should equal one genius of a girl in math!

"I'm waiting," Carl said, patiently sucking on his candy. He took it out to see how much was left, then put it back and licked his sticky fingers.

"Carl, sometimes I think you are really an old man in disguise," Toni said. "All right, you want to know what made me cry? I'll tell you. I failed the math test. Daddy and Mama are mad at me. I fell on your stupid toy. Susan hasn't answered any of my letters. Mattie doesn't like Susan. I'm scared I won't get into King Academy, and I'm not even sure I want to go. There, does that satisfy you?"

"Yes," he said. He kissed her cheek and left.

Strangely enough, Toni felt better. Mr. Ashby wasn't anybody to fool around with. If he said the test had to be corrected, then she'd better finish those last four problems, whether she wanted to or not. Fortunately the hall was deserted, and she got to the bedroom without meeting her parents.

Toni closed the door quietly. Her room was small, with just enough space for her bed, desk, bookcase, chair, and chest of drawers. It wasn't fancy like Susan's, which had coordinated colors and a stereo set. The window in front of the desk looked out on the backyard. And on top of the desk sat her music box, a gift from her grandmother. Some nights she enjoyed touching the water lilies painted on the top and hearing the childlike song.

All of her schoolbooks were scattered over her desk. Toni selected what she needed. An hour passed while she rested on her knees at the side of the bed, wrestling with subtracting fractions with different denominators. Then the room darkened, and Toni realized that it was time to help with dinner.

After dinner Toni returned to her homework, while her mother kidnapped Carl for a bath. She saw her father disappear into the kitchen. He was preparing to become a certified public accountant and had to study for his own exam in May. He was enrolled in a six-month review course, which meant that he often came home late.

I'm not getting this, Toni thought after twenty minutes. *Better call Mattie.*

"Mattie? Hi, me. I'm stuck on number four."

When they had finished correcting the exam, Toni yawned. She lifted her hand to muffle the sound. Her right arm brushed her tender breast. Toni thought this might be a good time to tell Mattie about her fears. It would be much easier with Susan, but she wasn't back yet. Talking with Mattie was worth a try.

"Uh, Mattie, does your chest ever hurt?"

"What do you mean? Like when I get a cold?"

"No, your breasts. Mine hurt," Toni explained.

There was a long silence.

"Haven't you noticed that I don't have anything there, Toni? So I'm the wrong person to ask," came Mattie's brisk reply.

"Oh." Toni heard the tightness in Mattie's voice.

"Did you hear from Susan yet?"

"No. She's probably busy with her father. I guess there's a lot to do in New York. Mattie, why don't you like her?"

"She's always acting like something thrilling and marvelous is happening to her, pretending, making up stories," said Mattie. "I don't know. She's never serious. What are her goals? Buying new clothes? Listening to records?"

"What's wrong with having a lot of energy and dreams?" argued Toni. "And imagination and wanting to have fun! It's that she likes boys and you don't!"

"Look, Toni, I don't hate Susan or anything like that. I don't even really dislike her," Mattie said, her words coming slowly. "Sometimes she's even funny. Remember that time we went downtown together and Susan made you pretend you were blind. That lady gave you five dollars!"

They both chortled, recalling Toni's shocked face.

"I was so scared." Toni giggled.

"So was I. There was a policeman right down the block!"

"So . . ." Toni waited.

"But you can't play games all the time! Last summer the director of the music camp said I have real talent! She told me that I could go to New York one day and study music. Maybe even win a scholarship!" said Mattie. "And I have to work hard to do that, because I don't have two parents, like you, or a family with money, like Susan's."

Mattie's last remarks jarred Toni. She hadn't thought about the situation that way. Why was it so easy for her to forget that Mattie's father had died only a year ago? Mattie was right. Susan's father and her grandparents did spend a lot of money on her.

"I just want us three to be friends and not have fights," said Toni. "That's all, Mattie."

"Look, I have to go. See you tomorrow, Toni. Bye."

Feeling pessimistic about peace between Mattie and

Susan, Toni decided to watch TV and forget about both of them.

"Honey, come on in the kitchen. Your father and I want to talk to you. I just put Carl to bed, so be quiet," called her mother.

I wonder what they want, she thought.

Toni didn't have to wait long to find out. She was grounded. No company, except to study; no going over to Susan's on the weekends; phone calls only about schoolwork; and she was to come straight home from school every day.

"How long?" asked Toni, staring at her father's set face.

"One month."

"Oh, Harold, that's too long. Why not make it two weeks, and then we can talk with Mr. Ashby?" said Mrs. Douglas. Her hand covered Toni's knee under the kitchen table.

Toni wished they wouldn't negotiate about her. But she played the game and added her appealing smile to her mother's.

"Whenever your mother and I try to help you with math, you get upset," Mr. Douglas said.

Toni nodded. That was true. Working with her parents made her feel even more confused. It wasn't their fault. She just felt so uncomfortable being surrounded by parents who knew all the answers when she didn't.

"Mr. Ashby told us to encourage you," her father continued. "Honey, maybe you want to work alone with me? You and I can set aside time each weekend to go over the problems you don't understand."

"No! I mean, no thanks, Daddy," Toni said. "I get too nervous. I promise to work hard. Really."

"All right. But we want better than passing scores, Toni," her father said.

Why do parents always want miracles? Toni thought.

2

One Problem Too Many

The rest of the week and the weekend dragged by with no sign of Susan. Toni studied with Mattie.

On Monday, after dropping Carl off at his side of the school building, Toni and Mattie hurried to their room. Mrs. Reynolds, the principal, was standing beside the classroom door with a strange white woman.

"Mr. Ashby's probably late," speculated Mattie, hanging up her faded denim jacket.

"We have that math quiz today," said Toni. "I'll forget everything by the time he comes!"

As the two girls sat down, the principal and the stranger moved to the front of the room. "Class, sit down and listen. Joseph, that means you," Mrs. Reynolds said.

Toni smiled. Mrs. Reynolds knew the name of every kid in the school. And she had earned the nickname "Radar" because she could detect trouble behind closed doors! It wasn't unusual to glance up in the middle of the day and spot Mrs. Reynolds at the back of the room, working with a kid.

"I have some sad news for you." Mrs. Reynolds spoke in well-modulated tones. "On Saturday afternoon, Mr. Ashby had a heart attack."

The class was silent, except for the clapping of a few hands. Mrs. Reynolds stopped it with one of her famous glares.

Toni heard shouts from all corners of the room. "Is he dead?" "Is he all right?" "When will he be back?"

Latwanda Morgan, a hefty girl with a deep voice, spoke out. "I saw my uncle die of a heart attack. We were all sitting around at my cousin's house, and he started choking and holding his chest. You know? Then he fell over. He died right there on the living-room floor."

For a moment the class was hushed. Suddenly, sparked by Latwanda's vivid description, other kids started sharing their experiences with death. Toni saw Mattie look down. Mattie's hands were shaking.

"What's wrong?" Toni asked.

"I don't want to hear all this. I really like Mr. Ashby. He's the best teacher I ever had," Mattie whispered. "And I don't want him to die, like my father did."

"He won't, Mattie." Toni didn't know what to say

to her friend. She'd never seen anyone die. Everybody she knew and loved was alive and well.

At that moment Mrs. Reynolds told the class to quiet down. Toni watched as the principal and the stranger restored order.

"Now that I have your attention again, I want to finish. Mr. Ashby is going to live. His wife told me that he will be just fine. But he won't be back for at least several months," said Mrs. Reynolds. The woman next to her smiled nervously.

"Oh, no!" exclaimed Toni. "He's got to come back!"

"But"—Mrs. Reynolds raised her voice—"we are very fortunate, because Mrs. Swallow will be replacing Mr. Ashby. She is an excellent teacher, and I want you to welcome her. Mrs. Swallow?"

The new teacher seemed to be in her forties. She was chunky and had pale blue eyes that protruded slightly. Toni noticed that her straw-colored hair was arranged in a loose knot.

Mrs. Swallow bent to retrieve a hairpin that had fallen. A plain wool skirt and white blouse completed the picture, except for something around her neck. Toni leaned closer to see. It was a ceramic necklace, and dangling down were bright orange carrots, green beans, miniature ears of corn, and slices of red tomato. On each ear Toni spied a ceramic carrot!

"Good morning, everyone. I'm sorry that this sad event has brought us together. But I'm sure we will have a good time and learn a lot," said the stranger, speaking quickly.

Astonished, Toni watched as Mrs. Reynolds left. Mattie nudged Toni, and they exchanged looks.

Mrs. Swallow told the students to bring their chairs to the front of the room and form a large circle. "But what about the desks in front?" asked Raymond. He stood in front of Mrs. Swallow, tall and straight. Toni watched. She liked the high, proud way Raymond held his head.

"What is your name?" said the new teacher, searching for Mr. Ashby's seating chart. "I guess I should have looked at this first. Uhm. . . . Ah, yes, Raymond Safford. Why, just push them back."

Toni and Mattie moved their chairs near the front of the room. Toni sat next to Raymond and pulled Mattie's chair next to hers.

"Where have you been going after school?" Toni whispered to Raymond. "I know you carry groceries on Fridays, but not the rest of the week."

Raymond leaned over and talked close to Toni's ear, so that no one else could hear. "That's confidential information."

Toni frowned, wishing that Raymond talked more. He had the irritating habit of saying only what was necessary, nothing extra.

"Raymond, come on, tell me," she said.

"Radar lets me use the computer room until she goes home. I'm writing my own programs," he replied.

"Programs to do what?" Toni asked.

"To do different things," he said.

Last year Toni and her classmates had been given three weeks of computer instruction. But this year, because of the shortage of machines, the sixth-grade computer classes had been postponed. Everybody had been disappointed, especially Raymond.

"And I'm saving money to buy my own computer and printer. With color graphics." He smiled and leaned back in his chair.

"But, Raymond, they cost thousands of dollars! It'll take you forever to save that much money," Toni said, checking to make sure the substitute was still busy organizing the room.

For a moment his confident face drooped. Then he straightened up. "I have time."

Toni winked at him. "Raymond, I believe you can get your computer and printer." He smiled back. But inside Toni sighed. The Safford family lived in a project. Raymond's father worked, but his mother was disabled from a factory accident, and money was always tight for them. At least Radar was letting him use the computers at school.

The stranger's shrill voice stopped Toni's thoughts.

"First we are going to play the Name Game, so I can learn all of your names and find out something about you. I'm Helene Swallow. I've been a teacher of first and second grade for ten wonderful years. You are my first upper-grade class!" She said the last sentence so quickly that Toni had to ask Mattie what she'd heard.

"We're her first sixth-grade class!" Mattie whispered.

"Does she know how to do our math?" Toni felt sick to her stomach.

"I don't know. Ask her," said Mattie, bending forward to catch the rapid bursts of speech that shot out of Mrs. Swallow's thin lips.

"And I'm going to do everything to make sure this is a great time for all of us," Mrs. Swallow concluded with a wide grin. "Now, I want the student to my right to begin. Your name is?"

"Latwanda Morgan."

"What a unique name. Now, Latwanda, I want you to tell me about yourself."

Latwanda's voice rumbled like an earthquake that measured 8.5 on the Richter scale. "Like what?"

"Latwanda, what are your favorite subjects? What are your goals for this year?"

The class snickered.

"Latwanda, go on. We're all ready to listen. Aren't we?" And she included each child in her nod of assent.

While Mrs. Swallow moved from student to student, Toni found herself paying attention. There were three kids whose names she didn't even know.

Before the class lined up for recess, Mrs. Swallow walked to the back of the room. Everybody turned around to see what she was going to do.

"Good. I've got your attention. When you return

from recess, I'm going to place you in groups of two. You and your partner are going to make a get-well card for Mr. Ashby. I will deliver our cards to the hospital today. One more thing: There will be no talking while you work together."

Still not believing what had happened, Toni let Mattie pull her into the line. Mr. Ashby was really not coming back. All through the rest of the morning and lunch, Toni was quiet. Then, after lunch, Toni got the answer she didn't want about Mrs. Swallow's teaching ability. She was sitting in her math group, next to Latwanda, while the new teacher rechecked the names of the kids before her. "Antoinette, your nickname is Toni and you like reading and writing and not math. Right?"

"Y-yes," stammered Toni, wondering why she was being singled out.

Mrs. Swallow beamed. "Well, upper-grade math is new to me, but I plan to take workshops to improve my skills. So we'll all learn together."

No! thought Toni in dismay. *She's not good at math! What am I going to do? Why didn't they send us a smart teacher?*

Toni jumped when Mattie pinched her forearm. She twisted toward Mattie, then stopped. Susan Lawrence strolled by, heading for Mrs. Swallow. She looked as if she were returning from an errand instead of a three-week absence. Susan grinned. She was the only girl in Room 308 who wore braces. Toni grinned back, taking in the way Susan's tawny brown hair bounced, the mischievous sparkle in her round eyes, and her new rust sweater-and-skirt set. The rest of the class called out to her.

Ten minutes later Latwanda poked Toni and passed her a note. She recognized the bright yellow paper. Furtively, with an eye on Mrs. Swallow, Toni tore the small gold seal and read the contents:

> Hi!!! Got back this morning. I have so much to tell you. Plus I have a surprise for you. Did you miss me? I missed you. S.

"What did she say?" asked Mattie, her face bleak.

Toni thrust the note into her purse. "Nothing much. Just that she missed me."

"Then why didn't she write?"

"Come on, Mattie! We'll find out after school. Don't get mad," Toni pleaded.

At the end of what had seemed a very long school day, Toni and Mattie waited for Susan outside the classroom. Mrs. Swallow was giving Susan the homework she'd missed.

Loaded down with books, Susan led the way out. "Hi, girl! Hi, Mattie!"

"Did you like New York? Why didn't you write?" said Toni, confronting Susan.

"I'm sorry, Toni. Mother Dear and Granddaddy got me at the airport. The plane was late, so we didn't get home until eleven this morning. New York is fantastic! I had the best time in the whole world! I want to live there! Be a famous model, wear beautiful clothes, and go out with rich men." As she spoke, Susan threw her free arm about in extravagant gestures.

"But why didn't you write me back? I wrote you four times."

"I said I was sorry." There was a tinge of impatience in her voice. "Look, I meant to. I just got so busy with Daddy. But I brought you a surprise and you, too, Mattie."

"What is it?" asked Toni.

"You'll see when you get to my house. Come on. You, too, Mattie," she said.

"No, thanks. I've got to baby-sit and study. See you two." And, with that, Mattie hurried away.

"What's with her? She's always saying she can't come. Anyway, let's get Carl and go to my house. Mother Dear was cooking and baking when I left. No telling what she's got ready for us." Susan tossed her head coolly.

"I can't. Daddy and Mama grounded me for two weeks," said Toni as they crossed the schoolyard. "I've got one week left."

"Why did they ground you?"

"I got a thirty on a math test, and you know how they are about me getting into King. I've been—"

"They'll never find out," Susan broke in. "Don't you want to see your present? Come on. You'll be home before anybody knows."

"What about Carl? He might tell."

"No, he won't. I know how to handle him." Susan laughed. Then, spotting him, she ran over to hug Carl.

"Susie! Susie! You're back! I missed you every day," Carl yelled, kissing her.

As they approached Susan's house, they were still talking about New York. Mother Dear was sweeping the front steps.

"Susan, I told you to wear a scarf before you went out of here," the small, sturdy woman admonished her granddaughter. "Get in here, you children, and let me look at you."

Toni smiled as Mother Dear embraced her, smelling like homemade rolls, apples, and cinnamon. Susan's grandparents owned a large, gray, two-flat building. They lived on the first floor, and a policeman and his family lived upstairs.

The front room was always so clean that it looked new. Pictures of Jesus and Dr. Martin Luther King, Jr., hung over the unused fireplace. Plastic covered the white brocade sofa and stuffed chairs. The coffee table and mantel were adorned with photographs of Susan as a baby, Susan learning to walk, Susan in a swing, Susan in every grade from kindergarten to fifth, Susan at Christmas, Halloween, and on her birthdays.

While Mother Dear steered Carl to the kitchen, Susan towed Toni into her room. Two single beds with matching comforters, drapes, and wallpaper, radio, color TV, and a stereo/cassette set completed Susan's bedroom. Toni loved the peach and light green colors.

There was even a door that connected Susan's bedroom to the bathroom—so Susan didn't have to go out to the hallway.

"Now, sit on the bed and close your eyes," Susan ordered, flinging her coat onto the floor.

Obediently Toni waited.

"Hold out your hands. Don't you dare peek!"

"Can I look now?" asked Toni.

"Yes. Come on, open it up," Susan said, her eyes happy and excited.

Toni did just that. The first thing she pulled out of a bag was wrapped in white tissue paper. It was a bra! A real bra!

"Do you like it? I guessed at your size, but Joanna, Daddy's girlfriend, said it should fit, and I knew you wanted one since I started wearing one and who knows when your mother will get around to buying you one," Susan said, the words spilling out.

"But what will Mama say if she catches me with this?"

"Does she watch you get dressed? No. So just be careful. Besides, wearing a bra helps the hurting."

"You know about that?"

"Sure. Mine still hurt sometimes. I put talcum powder and the bra on," explained Susan. "Mother Dear told me it's normal. They're just growing. Look at the rest. Quick, we have to get back in the kitchen. I don't want Mother Dear to see what I got you. This is our secret. All right?"

"Sure," Toni said.

Susan unwrapped a pair of earrings shaped like the Statue of Liberty, a poster of her favorite singer, Michael Jackson, and some postcards of New York. "I have some earrings like those, too. We'll start a new style."

Toni gazed at the postcards, stopping at one titled Greenwich Village. "Thanks, Susan. I didn't expect all this."

"That's where Daddy lives now with Joanna. She's not bad, just kind of spacy. Daddy's getting ready to make a record. I hope he makes a lot of money and then I can live with him forever," she said, her voice wistful. "See, I was thinking about you. Oh, I got Mattie something, too."

Susan got up and went to the bureau. "It's a T-shirt that says 'I Love New York!' I thought about getting her earrings like ours, but I knew she wouldn't wear them."

"Why did you buy all this?"

"I had a lot of time, and Joanna loves to shop. Plus I missed you."

"Children, come on back here and eat before Carl finishes up everything in sight," called Mother Dear.

Toni bundled up her gifts, feeling guilty for being so angry with Susan. Father Lawrence was sitting in the back room off the kitchen, reading the newspaper. He peered up over his glasses to greet Toni. His slender, lined face lighted up at the sight of his only grandchild.

"Hello, young ladies," he said in his formal manner.

"And how was school, sister? Now, wasn't it valuable for you to be there, if only for an hour? I'm going to have to talk to your father about yanking you out of school so much."

"Please don't, Granddaddy! I'll catch up, I promise," said Susan.

"We'll see." He returned to the newspaper.

The cuckoo clock in the hall sang out while they were eating. Toni hurried Carl into his jacket, and together they rushed home. Her gifts were securely held in her arms.

Mrs. Stamps and Hannibal were going up the stairs as they entered. Toni shot them a quick hello and grabbed Carl before he started playing. But it was too late, anyway. Her mother had already unlocked their door.

"Toni? Carl? What are you two doing getting home now?" Mrs. Douglas said, her eyes boring a hole into Toni. "Well, where have you been?"

"Susan invited us over for a little while," Toni began. "And I guess we stayed a little too long."

"Mother Dear gave me all the cookies I wanted," Carl said. "And I ate ten."

"I've got typing to do. But when your father and I say come home right after school, we mean that, Toni. And, Carl, eating ten cookies is nothing to be proud of," she said. "Toni, no more going over to see Susan. Remember, you are grounded."

Toni stared at her mother. She saw a frazzled woman with too many lines in her face, hurrying down the hallway to make a strong pot of coffee. Actually neither of her parents had much time. If her mother wasn't running away to type some student's paper in the bedroom, then her father was barricading himself in the kitchen to study for the CPA exam or coming home exhausted from class. And he had to juggle preparation for the May exam with his new job at an accounting firm.

Rushing after the retreating figure, Toni shouted, "But, Mama, I have to tell you about Mr. Ashby. He had a heart attack. We got a new teacher. Mama, she's not good in sixth-grade math!"

"Carl, don't turn that TV on!" yelled Mrs. Douglas. She snatched a large container of spaghetti sauce from the freezer. "Toni, about six P.M. put on some noodles, heat up this sauce, make a salad, and set the table. Your father is going to be late tonight." She poured some water in the coffee pot. "Now, what's this about a new teacher?"

Toni repeated her news, aware that her mother was not really listening.

3

Sixes and Sevens

The next morning Toni paused beside the mailbox two blocks from school to screw on the Statue of Liberty earrings. Carl ran ahead of her. *Susan's late, as usual,* Toni thought. Another ten minutes passed and no one showed up, so Toni went on to school.

After the Pledge of Allegiance, Mrs. Swallow had the class repeat the Name Game. Toni remembered the three names she'd learned yesterday. While the class was playing, Susan strolled in. This time the teacher told her to be quiet and made the class pay attention to the game.

Mrs. Swallow changed math to morning and called the low group together near her desk. Toni sat next to her teacher's desk, facing the rest of the class. Mattie and Raymond looked so secure in the top math group.

"Now I'm going to pass out individual chalkboards and chalk," said Mrs. Swallow. "Bring an old, spare sock tomorrow to keep your chalk in and use as an eraser."

"But this is for babies," said Latwanda, refusing to accept her materials. Her small, dark eyes defied the teacher.

"That used to be true, Latwanda. Now students in college use these," said Mrs. Swallow, gently thrusting a chalkboard into the girl's clenched hands.

Toni frowned. What would Mrs. Swallow come up with next? Toys to play with? Cute songs to sing in a circle? She swung her head around, causing each Statue of Liberty to sway back and forth. Susan was in the middle math group, working in the center of the room. Toni felt good when Susan looked up and tossed her head, too.

Armed with a large bag of lima beans and copies of the multiplication tables, Mrs. Swallow cornered Toni.

"But this is what first-graders learn with," Toni protested, feeling like Latwanda.

"We teachers all have our own methods. This is mine. Working with fractions that have different denominators requires a special kind of understanding." And with a firm tone, she issued a series of instructions that Toni had to follow.

On the chalkboard, Mrs. Swallow had written

"$1/2 - 1/6$." Under her careful eye, Toni placed lima beans on the blank sheet of paper before her, drawing a fraction bar to separate the numerator from the denominator. Then she read the multiplication tables for twos and sixes. Six was the common denominator.

"Good, Toni, you're trying," said Mrs. Swallow, shoving a hunk of hair back into a vague knot. "This is a hard one coming up, group, but you're all smart, and you can get the correct answer."

Toni selected lima beans for the numerators and denominators, consulted her multiplication tables, and counted out her lima bean answer. After writing the answer on her chalkboard, she caught Mrs. Swallow's attention.

"Good thinking, Toni! That's right. Now show me what you did."

Before the class was dismissed at the end of the day, a memo from the principal, Mrs. Reynolds, was given to everyone to take home. Buoyant from success, Toni simply folded the note and put it away.

Mattie's eyes were wide after she read her copy of the message. "The pretest for sixth-graders who want to qualify for special public schools is in seven weeks, Toni, just after Thanksgiving."

"It can't be that soon. Let me read that." Toni twisted around to see Mattie's note.

On the way out, Susan caught up with them. Then the three girls picked up Carl.

Toni studied the sky. It was now no longer blue,

but rather a sooty gray. Walker Elementary School blended into the dull sky. The old brick school building and fading foliage needed a facelift.

Toni thought of another school. King Academy was all new orange-red bricks and sparkling windows scrubbed to reflect the sunshine. Trees, manicured shrubs, and pots of colorful flowers adorned the grounds. Toni could see the autumn colors in her head. She wondered what King looked like on the inside.

"Toni! Didn't you hear me?"

"Hear what?" Toni mumbled. "Carl, put that hat on your head, not in your pocket."

Susan's hazel eyes danced. "Everybody in Ida's group wants to wear earrings like ours. Boy, is that Mrs. Swallow weird? She told me I need extra practice because I was absent. I can catch up any time I want to."

Mattie walked with Carl.

"Well, I can't. She may be strange, but at least I got some of the problems right today. Aren't you going to try to get into King with me and Mattie?" Toni asked, wrapping her scarf more tightly around her neck.

"I don't know. Who cares? That's too far away. Daddy wants me to come and live with him in New York. Just as soon as he finishes this record," she went on, waving at four girls who were bunched together like squashed daisies in a flower container. "See Ida and the others over there? You think I should tell them how to get the Statue of Liberty earrings?"

"What do you mean, you might live in New York? What about King?"

"Why are you so excited about going to King? Your parents want you to go there more than you do, Toni. Now, Mattie, that's different." Susan stopped and waited for Mattie. "She really wants to get into King. If I get in, fine; if I don't, fine."

The sound of her name made Mattie look up. But she said nothing. Carl broke away from Mattie and ran up to Susan.

"Susie, can I get more cookies today?" he pleaded, making his eyes big.

"Sure."

"No, Carl. We have to go home. Are you really going to move to New York, Susan?"

"I don't know, Toni. Maybe." The bounce in Susan's step flattened into a slow drag. "Daddy and I didn't spend too much time together. He was busy making a record and stuff. So I was with Joanna a lot. But that's going to change when he makes that hit album."

Mattie shot Toni a frown.

Toni ignored her. "Then why did you stay there so long?"

"He kept promising that we'd spend the next day together. Anyway"—her voice lifted to a forced high— "I had a lot of fun and can't wait to get back. By then Joanna will be gone. They fight all the time. I know he doesn't really like her."

By this time they were at the mailbox that served as the meeting place for the girls. Years ago Toni and Mattie had agreed to meet there, since it was located between their homes and school. Since Susan's house was only three blocks from Mattie's, it was convenient for her, too. Mattie left to baby-sit, and Toni watched Susan drift down the street, bright as any newly fallen autumn leaf.

Over the next week and a half, Toni vacillated between trying to achieve in school and wanting to give up. Mrs. Swallow's reports about Mr. Ashby's improved health cheered the class. Especially Toni. Maybe he would come back sooner and things would be normal again.

Raymond called Toni on Sunday afternoon.

"Hi, Raymond. I didn't see you in church," Toni said.

"Had to work. You want to go to the show with Gina, Paula, and me? Bring Carl, too."

"What are you going to see?" Toni asked.

When Raymond told her, she was excited. It was just the space adventure that she wanted to see. Quickly Toni asked her parents, knowing they'd agree when she volunteered to take Carl and that her father would give her extra money for hot dogs, candy, ice cream, pop, and buttered popcorn. Carl loved to eat at the show.

The movie was thrilling. The kids cheered, clapped, screamed, and laughed. During the walk home, Toni and Raymond strolled together. Gina, Raymond's older sister, held on to Carl and Paula.

"Raymond, what do you think about Susan?" Toni asked.

"She's like a good computer program with bugs—mixed up," he said slowly.

"Darn, Raymond, you sound critical, just like Mattie."

"That's okay. You asked me what I thought, right?"

"I just want the two of them to be best friends. Then we can all be best friends together," Toni said.

Raymond stopped and looked at her. "If you can do that, you can make my computer appear. Abracadabra!" Laughing, he tagged Toni and ran down the street past his sister and the little kids. Toni flew after him.

The next Friday was Halloween, and Susan was giving a party. Toni and Mattie had both been invited. And since it was on a Friday night and at Susan's house, they could go.

Toni wondered if her gypsy outfit would look good. Her mother had bought her a red cotton blouse and let her borrow a ruffled taffeta skirt, gold scarf, and all of the costume jewelry she could get on. Mattie was going as a nurse. Susan had kept her costume a secret, dropping hints now and then.

Knowing how nervous parties made her, Toni decided to take a bubble bath. Somewhat more relaxed after the bath, she fastened the bra that Susan had brought her from New York. Toni turned around, enjoying the way she looked in a real bra. Then she noticed something on the inside of her thighs. It was blood! Befuddled, she tiptoed to the toilet and sat down, wiping at her thighs with a damp wash cloth.

Oh, no, my period! What do I do? Maybe I'd better call Mama. No, I can't! Mama's out with Carl, trick or treating. I don't want to tell Daddy. Calm down, Toni, don't panic.

Despite the shock of seeing the blood, Toni was able to gauge that the flow was light. So she placed a wad of tissue between her legs. Stooping down to search for her mother's sanitary napkins, she felt a surge of gratitude. On a hot Sunday last August, when just she and her mother were home, they had talked about her growing up, starting her menstrual cycle, and learning how to change her napkins and keep herself clean.

Recalling every step, Toni peeled off the paper that covered the adhesive strips and pressed the napkin to her panties. When she pulled her panties up, the way her mother had demonstrated, she shifted around, unaccustomed to the bulk of the napkin. Then she wrapped two other napkins in tissues to put in her purse.

Tiptoeing down the hall, Toni reached her room and put on her costume. Her hands were shaking, and she felt she had to talk to somebody. Her mother would be gone for another hour. She couldn't talk to Susan on the phone; her father would hear. That left one person.

Toni found her father working in the kitchen.

"Daddy, I'll be back in a minute," she said. "I have to see Mrs. Stamps."

He looked up and smiled. "You look so pretty, honey. Just tell me when you're ready to leave."

"Okay, Daddy."

One foot tapped the rug as Toni pressed Mrs. Stamps's doorbell, praying that she was home.

"Toni my dear, have you come trick or treating?" Mrs. Stamps asked.

"Oh, no. I need to talk to you."

"Fine, come in, my dear. Hannibal and I were just watching television. You look like a real gypsy! I like you in red."

Relieved, Toni stood in the hallway until Mrs. Stamps took her arm and led her to the sofa.

"Something has happened and Mama's taken Carl out trick or treating and Daddy's upstairs. But I can't tell him," Toni said, holding her legs tightly together.

The old lady sat close to Toni, patting her hand and listening.

"I have to go to Susan's Halloween party. Mattie's waiting for me and Daddy to pick her up. I was in the bathroom getting ready to go and—" Toni couldn't go on. She looked away.

"And your menstrual cycle started?" Mrs. Stamps asked, her voice tender.

Toni nodded. "I did just what Mama told me to do, but how can I go to the party now? What if somebody can tell? What if something shows?" Toni asked. "I'm scared to walk. I can't dance."

"Why not? You are going to be fine, Toni my dear. Having periods is normal. No one will be able to see anything. You don't look different to me," she said. "Nothing shows."

"Are you sure?" Toni stood up and turned around slowly.

"I have twenty-twenty vision and I can't tell that you are menstruating. All I see is a lovely gypsy. As long as you carry extra sanitary napkins, you can change whenever you need to."

" See, I have two extras wrapped in tissues, just like Mama told me," Toni said, taking the sanitary napkins out of her purse.

"I just bought a cosmetics bag that would be perfect for holding your napkins. Then you can open your purse and keep your privacy." Mrs. Stamps got up and came back with a small bag, the size of a fat envelope, decorated with green and pink stripes.

"Thank you, Mrs. Stamps. That helps. They fit just right." Toni grinned.

"You're welcome. My, Toni, it has been such a long time since I had a period. I do remember that I danced until dawn, drove cars, and rode horses. In fact, I did anything I wanted to do, period or no period," she said.

"You did?" Toni asked. "What about boys? Can they tell?"

"They can't detect anything unless you tell them.

Now, I want you to go to the party and have a wonderful time." Mrs. Stamps hugged her and kissed her cheeks.

"Okay, Mrs. Stamps, I'll try," Toni said.

During the car ride to Mattie's and then to Susan's party, Toni held on to Mrs. Stamps's words. She squared her shoulders as she and Mattie entered the noisy wood-paneled basement where the party was under way.

The twelve boys and girls Susan had invited milled around in tight groups of two or three, some near the record player and others near the punch bowl, hot dogs, and potato chips. Raymond had transformed himself into a rock star. Toni smiled, clutching her canvas purse close. Mattie hung back.

Toni stopped and caught her friend's cold hand. Then, self-consciously, they crossed the room, heading toward Susan and almost forgetting to say hello to Mother Dear, who was chaperoning from a chair in the corner.

"Hi, girl. Hey, Mattie Benson, R.N.," Susan called, flouncing away from Ida. "Did you wear the false eyelashes? Oh, I guess not."

Susan was resplendent in a long, apricot organdy dress with bows on the shoulders and a stream of apricot, white, and yellow ribbons down the back. She carried a white cane.

Suddenly Toni felt ridiculous, with six bracelets on each arm, necklaces draped around her neck, and those

Statue of Liberty earrings. Why wasn't Susan wearing hers?

"Hi," said Toni, needing to escape to the bathroom.

"That's some outfit," commented Mattie, who looked crisp and professional in her nurse's hat and uniform. "Where did you get it, Little Bo Peep?"

Susan twirled around. "Joanna gave it to me."

"That's nice," Mattie said and went to get a hot dog.

"Why aren't you wearing the earrings? I thought we were supposed to wear them everywhere," whispered Toni.

"They didn't look right with this."

"I have to talk to you. Come on to the bathroom with me," Toni said.

"I can't leave my party now!"

Toni grabbed Susan's arm and pulled her upstairs to the bathroom.

"Okay, okay, we're here. What's the big emergency?"

"I got *it*," Toni said, locking the door.

"It? What's it? Come on, we'll miss my party."

"What you got last spring."

"You mean you got your period?" asked Susan in a shocked voice. "Are you sure?"

"Don't be dumb! I'm sure."

"That's amazing. How do you feel?"

"Different. I don't like this, Susan. My stomach hurts, down here." Toni pointed to her lower abdominal region. "And the sanitary napkin feels real strange.

Can you see anything? I mean, can you tell? I'd die if anybody could tell!"

"Nope."

"I don't like walking."

"Don't worry. I've had seven so far. Did you bring some extras? Mine wasn't much the first two times. You want an aspirin?" she asked. "Mother Dear gives me tea with honey and puts the heating pad on my stomach. You know, here."

"I brought two napkins with me, see?" Toni showed her friend the cosmetics bag. "How do you keep from—I mean, how do you know when to change, so nothing happens?"

"Well, at first I looked all the time, every hour. But it depends on how fast you flow. Just check yourself." Susan opened the door. "Now we're both grown. You coming?"

"In a minute," said Toni. "Thanks for helping me."

Susan paused in the doorway, the light from the bathroom and the hall flowing around her. "I'm your best friend, right?"

"You sure are," said Toni. "Tomorrow we go to Water Tower Place." Secretly glad that Mattie had to work, Toni was excited about spending a day alone with Susan. They'd have fun.

"Tell your mother that we're going to the library. We will. Then we'll head downtown." The door closed.

Toni could hear snatches of party music and the

sounds of dancing. *If Susan can handle this, so can I.* With a flourish, she marched out.

'Hi, Toni. I like your costume."

Surprised, Toni looked up to see Raymond standing in the hallway. Against his reddish-brown skin, the purple shirt, gold chains around his neck, and black pants looked good. His dark eyes glowed.

"Oh, hi!" Toni's face flushed. "You look sharp."

"I was coming as a computer chip, but Paula pulled out the wires I'd glued. You're a gypsy, right?" he asked, relaxed and calm. "I was looking for you. Want to dance?"

Toni frowned. She and Raymond had been comfortable friends for years and now, tonight, she felt awkward.

"I don't think so, Raymond. I don't feel good," she said. Hoping that Raymond couldn't tell what was going on, she leaned against the wall. After all, he had an older sister.

"You got the flu?" he asked. "Gina and Paula got sick this week."

"I don't know. I just feel tired." she said.

"If you feel like dancing, just tell me," he said, walking back with her to the party.

Grateful for Mattie's company, Toni sat out the rest of the party, watching the boys wolf down hot dogs and punch one another. Some of the girls danced together.

Toni glanced at Mattie. "You don't have to sit with

me. Don't you want to dance?"

"Not really. I'm just not ready for all this party stuff. But it's interesting to come and watch," Mattie replied.

"Oh."

Toni wanted to go home. She probably wasn't ready for all this either. In fact, she was "feeling all sixes and sevens," an expression Mrs. Stamps used when life upset her. "I don't feel good."

"Want me to call your father and have him come and get us?"

"Is it all right with you if we leave?" Toni asked.

"Sure." Mattie got up to call.

But it was Toni's mother who came to get them instead of her father. "What's the matter, honey? You were so eager to go," she said, opening the car door as Toni eased in and Mattie followed.

"I just have an upset stomach," Toni lied. During the ride home, she shut her eyes.

In the peace of her room, Toni hung up her costume. Then she put on a robe and went to the bathroom to wipe off the mascara, rouge, and lipstick from her face. After she'd checked herself, Toni brushed her teeth.

The hallway was dark and still as she made her way to bed, but Mrs. Douglas was in the kitchen, beckoning to her. Two cups of cocoa had been set out on the kitchen table.

"You don't get upset stomachs, Toni Douglas. What's going on?" Her mother's voice was low and gentle. Mrs. Douglas's soft eyes settled warmly on her daughter's face.

Toni squirmed in the wooden chair, spilling the cocoa.

"Well . . . you know what we talked about last summer?" she began, stopping to slurp the cocoa in the saucer.

Mrs. Douglas leaned her chin on her hand and thought. "You are becoming a young woman. Right?" she asked, her hand grasping Toni's.

"Yes, Mama. It started . . . I mean, my period started and I did everything you told me to."

"Oh, honey, and I wasn't here to help you. Why didn't you talk to Daddy? He understands all of this, Toni. Don't be reluctant to turn to him if I'm not here," she said. "Do you want the heating pad? Some hot tea with honey? Aspirin? Exercise will help the cramping."

Toni laughed. Mothers and grandmothers weren't all that different.

Saturday was a busy day. Toni's parents holed up to study and type, while Carl left happily to spend the weekend with his pal, Harry Edwards.

Warm in jeans, a green wool sweater, socks and boots, and a jacket, Toni walked the four blocks to Susan's. The trees stood lean and ready. Leaves swirled on the ground. The sky seemed feathered with cloud tufts.

Toni found Father Lawrence playing dominoes in the back room with Mr. Captain, his old war buddy. Mother Dear was at church. And Susan, dressed exactly like Toni, was ready and waiting. She was exuberant. The party had been a major triumph. Three of the girls had already called to tell her so!

Strutting down the street, Toni and Susan breathed in the chilly air and laughed. Their matching Statue of Liberty earrings shook in the wind. Catching each other's arms, chortling at everything they saw, the two girls soon reached the small, worn neighborhood library. Toni immediately found the books she needed to complete her social studies report on Brazil. Before she could check them out, Susan hauled her over to the reference section.

"Look, I found a book on what names mean. Like your name, my name," she said, excitedly thrusting a medium-sized red book into Toni's hands. "Susan is from the Hebrew language and means 'a lily.' I like that. I'm a flower. There's a beautiful picture of all kinds of lilies in the encyclopedia. See?"

"What does my name mean?" Toni said, plunking down at a table. "Antoinette. Wow! It's French and means 'inestimable.' Susan, what does that mean?"

"Do I look like a dictionary? Do what Mr. Ashby always says. 'Follow the guide words and look it up,' " she said, getting up for the large reference dictionary.

Toni pointed to the word. "There it is."

"Listen to this, girl. You are something else!" Susan said. " 'Inestimable' means 'incapable of being estimated or computed.' And definition number two says 'too valuable or excellent to be measured or appreciated.' "

"I like that last one. My name means that I am too valuable to be measured. You can't reduce me to my lowest terms!" said Toni. "What about Carl? And Mattie?"

"One at a time. Carl is from the Teutonic. I don't know that word. And it means 'robust and manly.' "

They laughed when they'd looked up *robust*.

"The only part of Carl that's robust is his appetite." Toni giggled.

"Now let's find Mattie. Hey, there's no Mattie. There's a Matthea. That's Hebrew and means 'gift of God.' That's nice. And there's Matilda—that strange word, *Teutonic*, again—and that stands for 'mighty battle maid.' That's Mattie, all right!" Susan whooped.

"I like 'gift of God' better. I'll call her later and tell her. Wait, let me write them down so she can choose the one she likes. I should look up Raymond, too."

"No, we don't have enough time. We'll be in this boring library all day. We can come back next weekend," Susan said.

Realizing that they both had to be home in a few hours, Toni hurried to copy down the information and check out her books so they could leave the library. Then the girls caught the El train downtown and the bus to Water Tower Place, a beautiful building with a waterfall and pots of blossoms. Eight stories of shops selling soap, food, furniture, tobacco, furs, and clothes! They rode the glass elevator, exclaiming as they swooped three stories up, then five stories down.

In one fancy shop, Toni tagged along as Susan selected four sets of skirts and sweaters to try on. A saleslady showed them to the dressing room, counting the items before they went in.

"I wish they wouldn't count. Then I'd take one." Susan shrugged off her clothes and stepped into an amber suede skirt.

"Susan! You might get caught! They'd call your folks and take you to the police station," Toni said.

"Not all the time. When I was in New York, I saw Joanna snatch two pairs of gold earrings and a silk scarf. Nobody arrested her!" Susan's face glowed.

"She did? That's awful. She's grown. They could send her to jail," said Toni, not wanting to hear any more. But Susan was not finished.

"You know those earrings I brought back? . . ." Susan paused, her face full of secrets.

"No! She stole these?" Toni felt her face flush as she saw the earrings in the mirror.

Susan pulled on a white cashmere cowl-neck sweater. "No, she dared me to try it. I did and guess what? I took two pairs, one for you and one for me."

Toni's voice squeaked. "The T-shirt for Mattie, too?"

"No, I didn't have the nerve to take that. Paid six dollars for it. You like this combination?" She whirled around.

The three-sided mirror cast back the dismay on Toni's face. "Susan, please don't steal anything again.

Daddy told me about what happens if you steal. He said if there was anything that I wanted that much, to come to him or Mama and talk to them about it." Toni pinned Susan with her words. "He said they would be so disappointed and ashamed of me."

"Hey, come on, Toni. Stop being so serious. I'll never do it again. I just told you because you're my best friend. This is our secret, right?"

Toni's full mouth narrowed. "Only if you promise not to ever steal anything ever again, Susan."

"I promise, I promise. Now, do you like this skirt or not?"

Toni touched her earrings. She didn't want to wear them again. But she couldn't tell anyone why.

They decided to stop for lunch. Not feeling as hungry as usual, Toni ordered a cheeseburger and a Coke. She searched for the aspirin her mother had given her to take for cramps.

"Too bad we can't eat at a real grown-up place," Susan said. "I did in New York. One night my father took me to a deli. Joanna was gone somewhere. I liked the deli. They have sandwiches and stuff, real sophisticated." Susan's face was alive with the memory of that evening. "He ordered chicken soup, a pastrami sandwich on an onion roll, and breadsticks with sesame seeds on them. So I did, too. We talked about his music. Toni, you know what? Daddy promised me that one day I'd live with him. Forever."

Seeing Toni's bewildered face, Susan paused, biting into her double cheeseburger. "What's the matter?"

"What's a breadstick?"

"Oh!" Susan laughed. "It's like a long, skinny brown cracker, kind of round. Sophisticated adults eat them. And alto-saxophone players like Daddy. I love them. That was our only time alone together. We walked all over the Village, talking and eating breadsticks."

Toni didn't know what to say. She was still shocked by Susan's confession. Father Lawrence and Mother Dear were the pillars of Ebenezer Baptist Church. They'd die if they discovered that Susan was a shoplifter. What had made Susan steal those earrings? As long as she'd known her friend, she had never taken anything.

"Do you know where we can find a deli?" asked Susan.

"I've never seen one in our neighborhood. I think there's one by the lake." Part of Toni wanted to talk to Susan about the earrings, but what could she say that she hadn't said already?

"I'm going to find a deli and buy ten packs of breadsticks. Then I can always have one," declared her friend.

"Why?"

"To remember that evening with Daddy. It was the happiest time of my entire life!" Then the laughter stopped. "I got a letter from my mother."

Toni put down her Coke. Susan's mother was a subject that she never brought up. Nobody did. Two years ago, when Susan's parents had divorced, her father flew to New York and his musical career, while her mother left her with her grandparents and took off. Toni had never met Mrs. Lawrence and didn't want to. Susan sometimes confided that her mother had called or written. Sometimes. Susan's mother was a touchy topic.

"Oh. Is she all right?"

"I guess so. She's living in Atlanta now and working for a TV station. Maybe I'll see her for Christmas," said Susan, her voice both hurt and wistful. "But I'd rather visit my father. He's the one who really loves me!"

"So do Father Lawrence and Mother Dear," Toni said.

"I know they do," Susan snapped. "After all, they *are* my grandparents!"

Toni sighed. She wanted to go home. There were times when being with Susan was such a strain. There were times when being with Mattie was boring. And now there were times when being around Raymond was uncomfortable. What was happening? Why couldn't Susan be more like Mattie? Why couldn't Mattie be more exciting? Shaking her head, Toni bit into her cheeseburger.

4

How Many Heartbeats?

Two weeks before Thanksgiving, Mrs. Swallow had the class working in groups of four to decorate the room. Raymond was in Toni's group with Mattie and a new girl named Helen.

Toni's group was assigned to make turkeys. Other kids struggled to cut the mammoth cornucopia that Mrs. Swallow wanted stuffed with paper fruit, nuts, corn, and other symbols of plenty.

"She really takes this holiday stuff seriously." Raymond was cutting around the tail feathers on a lopsided turkey.

They all laughed.

"You know who she reminds me of?" he asked Toni.

She nodded, still laughing.

"Miss Boswell." Raymond shook his head. "That teacher had us cutting all the time—turkeys, valentines, Christmas trees, alphabet letters," he said to the other kids. "Toni cut so much she got a blister."

"And when you saw the blister, you took all the scissors and hid them in the boys' bathroom," said Toni. "It took her days to find them."

"How many turkeys do we have to do?" asked Mattie.

Helen shrugged her shoulders and continued tracing turkeys from a pattern Mrs. Swallow had handed them. Her eyes were hidden by dark glasses.

"Who cares? Let's do as many as we can," Toni said, enjoying the respite from schoolwork. Cutting and joking with Raymond made the day pass faster.

When Thanksgiving morning finally arrived, Toni lay awake in bed, listening as her father got up early to cook his special blueberry-walnut pancakes. It was going to be a great day. The whole family and Mrs. Stamps were invited to the Lawrences' for dinner. Mattie would be going to her aunt's. And Raymond's family always went to the West Side of Chicago to spend the holiday with his grandparents.

Toni felt rested. The window overlooking the yard and alley below was fogged. But the room was warm. Hearing the hum and abrupt rattle of the radiator, she was glad that one of her parents had turned it on during the night. After a long, relaxed stretch, she went to get Carl up. His arm was draped around his orange stuffed giraffe. The covers were tousled, leaving his right leg uncovered. Toni shook him awake gently. Delicious smells would be coming from the kitchen soon, and she was ready for a stack of Daddy's pancakes with sausage.

The rest of the day was lazy and restful. They were due at the Lawrences' at 4 P.M. At about three forty-five the family picked up Mrs. Stamps, who looked elegant in her mink coat and matching hat. She accepted Mr. Douglas's arm as he led her to the family car. On a cold day like that, Toni was glad they weren't walking.

Carl tugged fitfully at his one good suit, while Toni smoothed the folds of her wool pleated skirt and yellow sweater. She touched the pearl necklace and tiny pearl earrings her parents had given her for her last birthday. The Statue of Liberty earrings lay in the back of her bottom drawer, wrapped in a tissue. She hoped Susan wouldn't ask her about them.

Father Lawrence opened the door, dapper in his starched white shirt, wool vest, and tailored slacks. Toni heard Susan calling her from the back of the house. She laid her coat on the big four-poster bed in the Lawrences' bedroom and ran to the kitchen.

"Hi! Come on and help me," said Susan, standing behind an oak worktable. Mother Dear commanded the area in her colorful turkey apron.

Toni cut the apple, pumpkin, and mincemeat pies, while Mother Dear checked the homemade rolls and basted the huge turkey. On every burner simmered a good-smelling pot. Toni's stomach rumbled. She hadn't eaten since breakfast.

"This is heaven. If Mrs. Swallow wants to see a real cornucopia, she should come to Mother Dear's kitchen on Thanksgiving! Everything smells wonderful!"

Just before the family and guests sat down to dinner, the phone rang. Father Lawrence answered it. He called Susan to the phone, telling her to take the call in her bedroom. Susan waved to Toni to join her, whispering, "It's probably Daddy. You can say hello to him."

But the caller wasn't Susan's father. It was Susan's mother. Toni sat uneasily on one of the twin beds and surveyed the room. There was something sticking out from the top of the dresser. She got up and lifted down a package.

These must be breadsticks, she thought. *They look like long cigars.*

Susan's side of the conversation consisted of one-word responses and lengthy silences. Finally Toni heard her murmur, "I have to go. Bye, Mama."

"You ready to eat?" asked Toni, putting the breadsticks back.

"I'm not hungry."

"What's the matter?"

Susan sat down beside Toni. Her face was tight and sad. "Why does she have to call and spoil everything? Why? Why, Toni?"

"I don't know, Susan," Toni said. "She misses you, I guess."

Her eyes blazed. "Then why did she leave me? Why

did she run off to Atlanta alone? I wanted to go with her!"

"I don't know, Susan. I'm sorry," Toni said. "Let's just forget about her and go eat Thanksgiving dinner."

Toni pulled Susan up, knowing that some things weren't easy to forget. Like the pretest for the entrance exams to get into King Academy. Maybe Susan didn't care, but she did. The pretest was in five days.

Toni reread the math word problem for the fifth time. Glancing anxiously at the clock in the front of the room, she forced herself to concentrate on the pretest. Time was running out.

Where am I? Yeah, here, number seven. Better read it again, thought Toni. *"Jason has saved $80. He sees a bicycle that costs $90 on sale for 25% off. How much money will Jason save by purchasing the bicycle at the sale price?" Who cares?*

Toni wrote, erased, and subtracted pairs of numbers. Discouraged, she read number eight, which was about slow and fast boats going so many kilometers per hour.

What's a kilometer? Toni sighed, feeling her stomach heave with tension. She gazed about her.

Steadily working through each problem, peering up as if out of a fog to pinpoint the amount of time left, Mattie was oblivious to her. Raymond was sharpening a pencil. Susan had finished and was reading a romance book inside her speller.

Mr. Ashby would have caught her, thought Toni.

Then she realized that Mrs. Swallow had positioned herself behind Susan. She took the book from her.

The clock on the front wall sped forward, never pausing. Lost amid planes and trains, watts and kilometers, radii and circumferences, Toni's heart sank.

By the time Mrs. Swallow collected the tests, she was near tears. Immediately asking to be excused, she retreated to the girls' bathroom and wiped her face.

I did better on all the computation. But those word problems! I can't figure out what to do! She looked at her tear-stained image.

"How did you do?" Mattie asked when she returned.

Toni told her.

"Then we just have to work on the word problems. I missed some of them, too," Mattie admitted.

"Me, too," Raymond added. "Don't worry, Toni. You'll get into King to please your parents and I'll get in to study computers. As for Mattie, she'll become King's lead singer, and Susan, well, Susan'll get in to flirt and play."

Everybody laughed except Toni. Not even Raymond's sympathetic smile dissolved the knot in her stomach.

Feeling as cold as the tiny wet snowflakes that clung to her face, Toni moped behind Mattie and Susan when they left school for the day. She spied Carl running around like a puppy, flinging his arms up to catch the snowflakes.

"That was a hard test," said Susan, shaking the snow out of her hair. "I tried, but there was a lot that I got stuck on. So I just stopped. No sense in giving myself a headache about a dumb pretest."

Toni's face was glum. "I kept going, but I don't know what good it did."

"Susie, let's play in the snow!" Carl yelled, dashing a few feet from her, then stopping to see if she would chase after him. When she did, he whooped and raced down the street, his scarf a bright green banner in the wind.

"Did you get the ones about percentages?" Toni asked Mattie.

"Yeah. If you estimated the number closest to ten percent, then took multiples of it, you could just mark the answer closest to that one," Mattie explained.

"How did you know that? Mrs. Swallow never taught us that," said Toni.

"I don't know. Just made sense to me."

Toni glared at Mattie.

When Toni and Carl got home, they knocked on Mrs. Stamps's door. Since their parents were both working late, they had been told to stay with her. Toni was glad. Being with Mrs. Stamps meant food, laughter, and peace.

"This is a perfect day for you two to be here! Just let me put on my exercise suit." Mrs. Stamps closed and bolted the door behind them.

One hour later they had devoured tuna sandwiches and chicken-noodle soup and hot cocoa. Holding a warm mug in her hand, Toni stared at Mrs. Stamps. She was dressed in a velour jogging suit and was pumping away on her exercise bicycle.

"A few more minutes and I'm through." She puffed, wiping her brow. Only the lines on her face revealed that she had lived for seventy-three years.

Carl played with his box of toys in the corner of the room. Engrossed in rediscovering a red crane that lifted small cars, he was lost in his own world. Toni envied him.

"So how was school today?" Mrs. Stamps said between labored breaths.

"Not good. I took the pretest to get into King."

"What's that?"

"They give us a pretend test to see what we need to work on for the real test."

"How smart! In my day you took the test and passed or failed. Not that I got to get much formal schooling. They didn't have many colleges for Negroes in those days. Except in the South, and I grew up in Detroit." Pump. Pump. Pump.

"I know I did well on most of it," Toni said, pouring some more cocoa from the teapot on the table. "But when I got to those stupid word problems, I messed up!"

"That's wonderful!" exclaimed the elderly woman, climbing off the bike.

"*Zoom! Zoom!*" Carl yelled, flinging a jet fighter into the crane, toppling it.

"Carl, keep it down to a soft roar, please," said Mrs. Stamps.

"Wonderful? Mrs. Stamps, I know that I failed that

part! This is *bad*. I'll never get into King Academy."

"You know what you did well on, don't you?" asked Mrs. Stamps.

"Yes, sort of."

"Then you know what you have to master in order to succeed." And, with that, she told Toni to do her homework, while she turned on the radio and started dinner.

Luckily her parents were exhausted when they got home that night. Toni managed to escape to bed without any unpleasant questions about the exam.

That week was the first in December, and by then the Christmas season was well under way. While Carl stayed home with his father, Mrs. Douglas took Toni Christmas shopping on the weekend. They drove to a suburb far from their neighborhood that boasted a beautiful shopping mall. Red, green, and white lights flashed in the cold air, cloaking the trees in garments less lush but more thrilling than summer's leaves. Huge candy canes, firmly strapped to metal posts, promised sweets and goodies. Shoppers scurried about from store to store.

"Oh, Mama, I love Christmas!" Toni cried.

"Do you have enough money to complete your Christmas shopping, Toni?" her mother asked.

"I've saved most of my allowance!" Toni replied proudly, visualizing the thirty dollars tucked away in her wallet.

After hours of searching through scarves, toys, stationery, and costume jewelry, Toni crossed the last name off her list and found her mother. Tired and pleased to have accomplished so much, they enjoyed a late lunch.

"How are you feeling?" asked Mrs. Douglas, looking closely at her.

"I'm okay," said Toni, chewing on a ham sandwich with extra dill pickles.

"Has your second period started yet?"

"No, not yet. I check every morning."

"Don't worry. Sometimes you miss when you first start, honey," she said. "I have something for you."

Her mother handed her a small bag. Toni unwrapped three bras, one white, one pink, and the other, blue. She didn't know what to say. Mrs. Douglas grinned.

"Yes, I know you're wearing a bra," she said. "Don't look so scared. I guess I've been too busy to notice that you needed one. Do your breasts hurt?"

Toni nodded.

"That's normal. Next time, tell me," she said, reaching for the check. "If they don't fit, we can return them. I know that I get busy, but what happens to you matters to me."

On Monday, before the results of the pretest were announced, Mrs. Swallow reported that Mr. Ashby was recuperating. Pleased but anxious, Toni crossed her fingers. Mattie had passed all the subtests with flying colors. Susan's scores were below grade level.

Nonchalantly she shrugged her shoulders. Raymond had scored high on everything except spelling. Toni was way above grade level on everything except for math. Her computation score was fair. But she had failed the word problem subtest!

"You've got a little less than four months to improve the computational part and learn how to solve word problems," said Mrs. Swallow, handing Toni a copy of her results to take home.

Toni tried to smile back, but she couldn't. Despite her disappointment, the school day went on, full of holiday activities. Dressed in something red or green, her class toured the primary classrooms, singing Christmas carols. Toni smoothed the red blouse and green ribbon tie she wore and ducked from embarrassment when Carl yelled, "That's my sister!"

Mattie's beautiful soprano had guaranteed her the lead slot. Toni's strong alto blended well with Mattie's voice. After all, they had spent many hours singing together in Ebenezer Baptist Church's Junior and Young People's Choirs, where Mattie had been a featured soloist for three years. Standing next to Susan, who was beautiful in her rich red velvet dress, Toni lost herself in the Christmas music. By the time they got back to the classroom, her earlier gloom had faded. Music was magic.

"Now, remember, I want anybody who forgot their trip slip to bring it tomorrow," said Mrs. Swallow. She was certainly festive in Christmas tree earrings, an angel brooch, and a red and green plaid dress.

The class groaned. Going to the Shanghai Museum Exhibition was not their idea of a sensational school trip. Not even Mrs. Swallow's films on Chinese art and folktale readings had ignited their interest.

Toni was different. She loved to go on trips. Her permission slip had been signed and turned in. On her way down the stairs, Toni's mind drifted to the up-coming weekend. Persuading Mattie to join her and Susan at the roller-skating rink on Saturday had been tough. But Toni had appealed to Mattie's sense of fairness and won. After skating, they were all going over to Susan's to listen to records.

What a wonderful Saturday we'll have! Sunday will be church, dinner, and maybe Daddy will take us to the show. The holidays meant fun, fun, fun! After Christmas would be the best time to worry about word problems and exams.

As they left school, Mattie called a quick good-bye before going to meet her twin brother, Matt. Mother Dear was waiting to take Susan shopping. Toni watched Susan stretch her long legs and toss her hair in the sunlight. Susan turned around and waved to Toni. Stamping her feet, Toni waved back. Then she began the trek home with Carl.

Three sixteen-story monolithic slabs—housing projects—lined the streets, blotting out the early-winter sunshine. Toni hated the projects. They were so ugly. It wasn't healthy to crowd hundreds of families into concrete prisons, with playgrounds the size of small backyards. Raymond lived in the project on the corner. Broken elevators, fires, and crimes were common. Kids and adults who lived in the projects and around them were scared of muggings, burglaries, even rapes. Toni sighed. She was glad that Raymond was smart and tough.

"Toni?" Carl tugged at her jacket.

"What, Carl?"

"Is Christmas tomorrow?" His gray eyes clung to hers.

"No! You ask me that ten times a day!"

"When is it?" he persisted, sucking on a lemon drop, not bothering to offer her one.

"In seventeen days. You know the calendar in the kitchen?" she asked, seeing him nod uncertainly. "The one by the refrigerator? We'll cross off each day, and I'll put a big *C* for Carl on Christmas Day."

Carl beamed.

"Do you need to see my list again?" he asked. "You promised to tell Santa Claus what I want."

"No. You showed it to me, and I know everything you want. So does everybody in Chicago. Including Santa and all of his reindeer!"

"What do I want most of all?" he quizzed, now handing her a lemon drop.

"A real bicycle with no training wheels."

"What color?"

"Carl." Toni drew out the one syllable into two distinctly unpleasant sounds.

"Red with black stripes! Remember." He ran ahead of her, adroitly evading a well-aimed pinch. "And a loud horn!"

Steering Carl down a street without a project on it, Toni rehearsed what she would tell her parents about the test results. As she turned the lock in the front door, she was filled with alarm. Her father stood in the hallway.

"Daddy! Why are you home so early?"

"I decided to take a personal half day off. So I closed up the accounts and came home," he said. "Hi, son. Yes, I know what you want for Christmas. I have your list in my pocket. Now scoot. I want to talk to your sister."

Toni hung up her coat and gave her father the results. She watched his thick black moustache shift as he scanned the piece of paper. Dressed in an old navy-blue sweater and cords, he looked younger.

"What do you think about this, Toni?"

"I really tried. Everything is up. The math is better. I just have to work on the word problems, but Mrs. Swallow said she'll help me and I have time," said Toni in an unrehearsed torrent.

He studied her for several minutes. "Honey, go and see if Mrs. Stamps will keep Carl for about an hour."

Puzzled, Toni obeyed and then took Carl downstairs.

When she returned, her father was dressed to go out. Soon they were driving through the streets. Toni hardly noticed the groups of young men warming their hands over small fires burning in metal trash cans, or the old man selling tangerines under the El train track.

Where is Daddy taking me? she wondered.

Her father parked the sedan in front of a large gray stone building with turrets and tiny windows. This was part of the campus of the University of Chicago. Taking her gloved hand in his, he led Toni through the portal in one building that opened out onto a garden surrounded by buildings.

Toni gazed around. As if reading her thoughts, her father took her into one of the buildings to the left and down aisles of books and long tables where people studied. Toni noticed that there were very few black students.

They continued walking around the campus. Her father finally stopped in front of a coffeehouse and opened the door for her. The room was filled with young whites, a sprinkling of blacks, some Asians. They were all laughing, chattering, calling to one another. Toni breathed deeply.

"Honey, what would you like? They have hot cider, hot chocolate, cake, cookies."

Toni decided on hot cider and spice cake. Feeling safe with her confident, handsome father, she enjoyed the guitar music and atmosphere. He had let her select a table by the window. They sat down next to each other.

"I guess you're curious about why I brought you to the university this afternoon," he said, sipping his hot drink.

"This is really something!" she said.

"Toni, our dream is for you to go to a fine university like this. Study. Learn. Get a good education. Join your friends at a place like this," he said.

"Sure, Daddy."

"No, you don't understand. You're black. You have to get a good education to make it in this troubled society, and sometimes even that isn't enough." He muttered the last part as if to himself. "Now, what you do with that education is your business, but your mother and I want you to have the tools to make a good future for yourself."

Toni drank her cider, nodding.

"I liked what we saw—the classrooms, lecture halls, and all those books! Everybody looked so serious in that library."

"One of several libraries," he said. "Yes, this is exam week; they'd better be serious."

"Can you learn how to be a writer or an actress here?"

"You sure can, honey. Or a lawyer, zoologist, doctor, physicist, teacher, anthropologist, mathematician—even an accountant!" He laughed.

"They must have a lot of teachers!" she commented, absorbing every detail of the coffeehouse so she could tell Mattie and Susan. *This is one place we've never been! Talk about sophisticated!*

"We have to leave soon and pick up your mother. She told me you're becoming a young woman." His smile was weary and a touch sad.

Toni's face flared, changing from bronze-colored to flushed red.

"That's wonderful, Pumpkin. I guess my baby girl is growing up." In a rare show of emotion, he hugged her.

"I feel funny, Daddy. Fine one minute, then strange the next," Toni said.

"Not unusual." He smiled. "So do I sometimes. About the test results, do your very best, Toni. Promise to really try, Pumpkin?"

Toni stared up into his face. Despite the softness in his request, his look was like steel. Pumpkin. That was her baby name. His hand squeezed hers.

"I promise, Daddy."

The next morning Toni maneuvered to the back of the public bus and staked out seats for Mattie and Susan. The Shanghai Museum Exhibition was at the Field Museum of Natural History. Toni had been there before, but as she strode through the tall columns, she felt a sense of awe.

Mrs. Swallow swooped around her class, shushing, throwing sharp looks, and organizing all twenty-six children into an attentive tour group. Then the docent, an elderly white woman, steered the class through antique statues, pots, bowls, and hanging scrolls, some over six thousand years old.

Susan giggled while Raymond and some of the other boys swung mock axes at each other, stimulated by the large bronze Yue axe blade on display.

"Quiet, now," said the docent, holding up her hand. "Class, what you are going to see next will astonish you. I want you to watch very carefully, because you will each have the opportunity to play with the Water Spurting Basin. Now, follow me."

Intrigued, the class watched as the docent showed them a shallow bronze basin. It had two hoop-shaped handles, and four carp in raised outline spouted imaginary water on the flat bottom.

"What's so special about this?" muttered Mattie.

"Come over here." The docent climbed onto a platform, where a replica of the basin rested on a wooden table. She filled the basin with clear water from a stone pitcher and then began rubbing the palms of her hands on the tops of both handles. The children buzzed as a high, droning sound filled the air. The docent rubbed the handles faster, maintaining a steady rhythm. Out of the bowl droplets of water leaped higher and higher. Magical spurts of water jumped up!

"Who would like to try?" she said.

Susan pushed ahead of Toni. Excited, she began rubbing the handles, producing the strange sound, which was followed by water spurting higher than before. Her delighted laughter flew out in peals, like the water. When Toni tried, she felt the same way. Even Mattie chuckled as her hands worked the magic.

Eagerly the class listened as the docent explained what made the water leap out of the bronze basin.

"Ming craftsmen were famous for their 'rippling basins,' bronze basins like the one you are enjoying. Now, quiet down and I'll tell you the secret."

"It's magic," Susan said.

"Well, not really. The phenomenon that makes the water leap up is called resonance, or sound vibration. When you rub both handles of the basin at the same time, you make the handles vibrate. When the water carries the vibration frequency to the sides of the basin, they pile up. When that frequency equals the frequency of the basin walls, the water jumps. When you rub more, the amplitude or fullness of the vibrations increases and the water gushes up."

"So rubbing the handles makes the basin vibrate, like the strings on a violin?" asked Mattie.

"Yes."

"And the powerful vibrations moving through the water make the water leap up?" Mattie continued.

"That's correct. And if you look closely, the water appears to be coming out of the mouth of the carp. That's because the Ming artists deliberately molded the mouth of each fish on the areas of the basin where there would be the greatest amplitude," she said.

After everyone who wanted a turn had had one, the docent led them to the final thrill of the exhibit, the Magic Mirror. Inside a display case was a round bronze mirror of a grayish color, mottled with patches of green and reddish brown. An elaborate raised design of symbols and whorls adorned the back of the mirror.

"This mirror does something quite remarkable. What it does is so amazing that Chinese scientists spent one thousand years trying to discover the secret of the Magic Mirror. Follow me." The docent led the sixth-graders to a much larger display case holding another Magic Mirror. A light in the case shone on the shiny bronze mirror surface so that there was a distinct reflection bouncing back on the case wall behind the light.

Toni angled her way to the front of the line. Something was strange. She saw on the wall the exact design that was visible on the back of the mirror. Somehow the mirror reflected the ornamental decorations that were on its back. But that was impossible!

Toni peered closely at the wall behind the light. Yes, there was the pointed star-shaped center of the bronze motif. Even the foreign writing that decorated the bronze back of the mirror was visible on the wall.

"That's weird," Susan murmured.

"What's that mirror made of?" Latwanda asked.

"The face of the mirror is a highly polished bronze," said the docent.

"How can a mirror reflect the design on its own back?" Toni faced the docent.

"That's the question that has taken a thousand years to answer, young lady. It's not really reflecting what's on the back of the mirror. It's reflecting the design on the shiny front of the mirror. This design is almost exactly the same as the one on the back. Though we can't see them with the naked eye, there are tiny ripples in the surface that were created during the casting of the mirror. When direct light or strong sunlight hits the shiny surface, the pattern appears and reflects off the mirror."

"I can't see any marks on the front of the mirror," Susan said.

"No, they are very small and you can't see them without special equipment."

While the docent answered questions, Toni, Mattie, and Susan stared at the display case. The class exclaimed when the docent explained that mirrors that reflected their own designs were thought to be able to predict the future and had been used in the past to heal the sick.

All the way back to school, the class talked about the exhibition. For the first time in ages, Mattie and Susan chatted amiably. Toni was pleased. It had been a great trip. And when all three girls walked to the mailbox together, still talking and joking, Toni knew that things were going to be better among them.

"Can you two come over?" asked Susan. "We can play records."

"Not me. Thanks, Susan, I have to work. See you later," Mattie said, smiling as she took off.

"Not today, Susan. But, remember, we'll spend all day Saturday together," said Toni.

"Okay. Wear your green sweater and jeans to school tomorrow," Susan ordered. "Then we'll match."

Toni grinned. "And our hair down and curled under."

"I like that! See you later." Susan waved good-bye. "Today was a lot of fun."

"See you tomorrow!" Toni yelled. Susan smiled.

5

Minus One

When Toni opened her eyes Wednesday morning, the sunlight streamed into her room. She was snuggled under layers of warm blankets and had to convince herself to hop out of bed and get ready for school.

When the telephone rang, Toni jumped. People didn't usually call that early. Holding one brown boot and wearing one, she hobbled to the bedroom door and looked out. Her mother had answered the phone.

"Oh, no. No! No! Oh, Father Lawrence. Jesus help us! It can't be true! Oh, Lord, no! No!" said Mrs. Douglas. "But the doctors . . . But how? . . . Why didn't you call us? . . . Yes, I understand. I'll come now. . . . Are you sure? . . . After work, then. . . . I know. Somehow we will. I'm so sorry. Lord. Lord." Mrs. Douglas let the phone drop and covered her face with her hands.

Before Toni could move, her mother rushed to her bedroom and slammed the door. Toni hung back. The conversation she'd overheard didn't make any sense, unless something had happened to Mother Dear. She had high blood pressure. Worried, Toni patted her hair and pushed up the sleeves on her green sweater.

Silence filled the hall. Toni listened to the muffled sounds of her mother crying and her father talking. Uneasy, she set the table for breakfast and stirred the Cream of Wheat. The bread stood poised in the toaster.

"Hey, Pumpkin, where are you?" came her father's voice.

"In the kitchen, Daddy," she said, taking the cereal off the burner.

She heard the rhythm of his stride. Mama's slippers flip-flopped behind him.

"Mama, why are you crying? What's the matter?" asked Toni. "Daddy?"

Toni waited, but they didn't answer her. Only the harsh tick-tock of the kitchen clock could be heard. She searched her father's eyes for a clue. They were so sad. Her mother's face was stretched taut.

"Honey, come on in the front room with us. Breakfast can wait." Her father clutched her hand tightly and led her to the sagging, butter-yellow sofa. Mama rubbed her other arm.

They're trying to give me something, holding me like this. Oh, I hope Mother Dear is okay. Susan would be so unhappy!

Her father stared at her mother, who gazed at the carpet. Toni heard him clear his throat.

"Damn, Dot," her father said, shifting his weight and standing up in the sunshine.

"Toni, honey . . . Uh, it was Father Lawrence who just called . . . and something . . . something tragic has . . . Harold, please help me." Mrs. Douglas turned to her husband.

"It's Mother Dear, isn't it? Is she real sick, Daddy?" whispered Toni.

"Oh, Pumpkin. No, not Mother Dear. As hard as that would be, this is worse." He stopped and bent down before her, taking her hands in both of his. "Honey, Susan died early this morning. She was killed by a car. The driver ran a red light."

Her mother's voice rushed in. "Susan was walking home from the store. Last night. The doctors tried, but— Oh, baby, they couldn't save her," said her mother, leaning against Toni.

The sunny room emptied.

"Susan? Su-Su—" Toni stuttered, shaking her head furiously. "Susan dead? Nope. It's a mistake, Mama. It's not true. I saw her. We went to see the Magic Mirror. Yesterday, Daddy. Yesterday."

"No, honey, it is true," Mrs. Douglas said, rocking her back and forth. "You are going to stay with me today. I'll call Professor Molinardi and let him know that I won't be in. Harold, sit with her. I have to check on Carl."

She got up. Toni felt her father reach out and hold her. She felt the weary creaking of the sofa. The aroma of his cologne, brisk and lemony, enveloped her. It had been a long time since her father had held her so closely.

Words floated in and out. *Susan. Car. Susan. Bang, bang. No. Bang, bang, ding. Dead friend. Susan dead. Bang. No.*

At some point during the day, Toni woke up. She dimly remembered undressing and going to bed, then darkness, oblivion. She was late. It was past time to go to school. She had to meet Mattie and— Her eyes jerked opened. In her mind she heard something, something horrible!

"Mama! Mama!" Toni screamed.

"Here I am. Everything's going to be all right. I'm here."

Toni clung to her mother's cool housedress. Her mother smelled like fried chicken and pie. Toni sniffed apples and cinnamon. *Like Mother Dear,* she thought.

"You're home, Toni. Home and safe," said her mother, smoothing the hair on her daughter's forehead.

"Susan? Mama, Susan?"

"She's gone, Toni. I know, I know. You slept most of the morning, and now I want you to eat. Mrs. Swallow called just a little while ago. She wants you to know that she will miss you today. How unhappy she is, and your classmates."

Toni stared away. Mama was saying that this morning was real. That Susan was dead. No, it couldn't happen. Not to her, not to Susan. No.

"Come on, now. Lying down with this kind of sorrow is no good. Get up. Let's get your robe on." Mama prodded, pulling back the covers. "Later on I'm going over to Mother Dear's and take the chicken and pie."

Robe, thought Toni. *Robe. Put on my robe.*

Mama held out the garment. Toni couldn't figure out where to put her arms. Finally Mrs. Douglas guided them into the sleeves.

Stumbling through the day, Toni moved her body jerkily from place to place. During dinner she noticed that Carl was sitting next to her.

Mama had cooked all of her favorites—fried chicken breasts, french fries with ketchup, salad, and apple pie à la mode. Toni put some of her french fries on Carl's plate, not knowing why. Her parents were saying something to her, but she couldn't understand the words. They floated past her like bubbles. After a few more attempts, they turned their attention to Carl and each other.

Toni's knife, fork, and glass weighed heavily in her hands. She saw herself slowly picking up and dropping the glass of milk. Her mother said nothing as she reached for a sponge and mopped it up. Toni watched, mesmerized. The milk was there, running into the dishes. Then it disappeared. Only a slightly sticky sheen remained.

"Dot, I'll go with you. Mrs. Stamps went over this morning. She offered to baby-sit the kids," said her father, pouring Toni more milk.

"No, Harold, I'd rather one of us was here. Reverend Webster will be there and others from church. I'll be fine," replied Toni's mother, rising to clear the table.

"Well, Toni, looks like it's you and me and Carl. Can I help you with anything? Your homework?" he offered.

Toni shook her head. The telephone rang. Thinking it was Susan, Toni ran to the phone and said, "Hi! I knew it was you."

But the voice on the other end was Raymond's.

"Toni? Mrs. Swallow told us about Susan. How are you doing?" he asked.

"Not good. Not good at all," Toni said, sinking into the chair. "What did she say?"

"That a drunk driver hit Susan last night. She was coming home from the grocery store. And she died."

"Oh."

"When are you coming back to school?" he asked.

"I don't know, Raymond."

"Toni, I'm sorry. I'll talk to you later. Bye."

"Thanks. Bye." She hung up the receiver and stood up.

Toni found herself in front of the bathroom mirror. The girl in the mirror was a stranger with red eyes, runny nose, matted hair, and swollen lips. The face in the mirror hurt. *Susan dead? No,* she said to that face. *On Saturday we're all going skating, all of us.* She started crying.

"Oh, Toni, please. Susan wouldn't want you like this." Her father stood in the doorway.

She pushed away the images of a body, a hole in the ground, a dumb angel. "Where's she gone to?" Toni choked out.

"Her body is dead. But her spirit is with God and with us, Toni," he said. "That's what you've been raised to believe."

"No, she's not dead. I want to see Susan! Daddy, stop this." Toni sobbed.

Mrs. Douglas came in with Carl in tow.

"What's the matter, Harold?"

Her father looked at his wife, then down at his grief-stricken daughter. "Dot, what are we going to do?" Toni was crying so hard her body shook.

There was no choice. On Thursday Toni had to go back to school. Her mother couldn't afford to take more time off from work. And Toni knew her parents felt that school was the best place for her to be.

Get up, put on my robe, be quiet, go to the bathroom, wash up, brush my teeth, get dressed, eat breakfast, help Carl, stack the dishes, get my jacket and Carl's. Make sure I've got my books. Run to meet Mattie and Susan by the mailbox—No, not today. Susan won't be there.

While she dragged herself through the motions, Toni's mind was blank. At the breakfast table, she poked at a bowl of steaming oatmeal, swallowing four teaspoons. Carl munched on his third piece of toast.

"Honey, I'll drive you two to school," said Mrs. Douglas, clearing the table with an eye on her watch.

Toni arranged her face in a wan smile. "No, thanks, Mama. We can get to school okay."

She was rewarded with a kiss. Her parents were concerned about her, but, at the same time, they depended on her to take care of Carl. Toni squeezed back sudden tears.

The route to school stretched endlessly. In the past couple of days, Carl had vacillated between frenetic play and glum silence. He was in one of his tongue-tied moods. When Ida and her pals called hello, Toni quickened her steps, taking Carl's gloved hand.

Automatically her eyes searched for a sign of Susan, half expecting to see that slender, bold face grin at her and hear Susan call "Toni! Toni!" They would strut the final blocks to Walker Elementary School— locked together, tighter than the tightest, secret sharers, best friends.

But only Mattie was there. Solemn, steady Mattie. Mattie, wearing last winter's jacket and lugging this year's books. In her mind Toni replayed Mattie's phone call after the announcement of Susan's death.

"Hi, Toni, it's me, Mattie."

"Hi."

"I heard about Susan today in class." Mattie had hesitated. "I hoped you'd come to school."

"Mama wanted me to stay home," Toni had said.

"I feel so bad, Toni. Lots of kids cried. Me, too."
Toni hadn't known what to say.

"I got your homework back and copied down the assignments for you, Toni," Mattie had said.

"Thanks, Mattie."

"When are you coming back to school?"

"Probably tomorrow. I don't feel good, Mattie. I can't believe it. I just can't," Toni had replied. "Thanks for calling. I have to go now."

Shaking herself, Toni returned to the present. Carl ran up to Mattie and hugged her. Startled, Mattie bent down to him. Toni mumbled a hello.

"Here," said Mattie. "This is the work you missed. Mrs. Swallow will let you make it up. I told her you and Susan are—I mean were—best friends." The words trembled out.

"*Are,* not were," Toni said. "We *are* friends. You talk like Susan is—" Unable to continue, Toni concentrated on the cracks in the sidewalk.

"I know," said Mattie sadly. "Dead is a hard word to say out loud. I still have trouble saying that word when I think about my father."

Noticing Carl's woebegone face, Toni took one of his hands and Mattie, the other.

Going upstairs to the classroom was easier. Everybody was pushing and gabbing. Toni and Mattie rounded the corner. There was Mrs. Swallow, wearing her Christmas jewelry with a red velvet blazer and skirt. Absently Toni wondered how many Christmas combinations her teacher could produce.

"Good morning, Toni. I'm glad you're back." Mrs. Swallow patted her shoulders vigorously.

"Good morning, Mrs. Swallow."

Heading for the coat rack, Toni avoided the furtive glances and hushed talk that pursued her. Mrs. Swallow had typed their names on blue plastic strips and taped them over the coat hooks. That eliminated all arguments about where the students hung their jackets or coats. Toni searched for Susan's strip, three hooks down from hers. Susan's name was gone.

She shoved past Raymond and Mattie. Kneeling down, she felt inside Susan's desk. It was empty! Books, papers, pencils, Susan's lemon-yellow stationery. All gone. The Big Time eraser, the one they had bought together to erase millions of mistakes. It was gone! *They stole her stuff! That's what they did!*

"Hey, what do you mean stealing Susan's stuff?" Toni screamed at the kids whose desks were clustered with Susan's—Ida, Helen, and Joseph.

"I didn't steal anything!"

"Me, neither."

"You better watch your mouth, Toni," Ida warned.

"Then where's Susan's stuff, you dirty thieves? Where's the stationery? Joseph, did you take the big blue pencil?" Toni balled her hands into angry fists.

"Nobody calls me a thief without a fight," Helen yelled. She jumped up and headed for Toni.

The class circled, sensing trouble. Mattie moved

over to stand next to Toni, her arm restraining her friend. Raymond ran between Toni and Helen.

"Don't you touch Toni. You hear me, Helen?" he said. Toni struggled behind him, trying to get at Helen.

"Toni, stop it. Helen, don't you move. I mean it," he ordered, still facing an angry Helen.

"What's going on here?" Mrs. Swallow's tone was controlled and cool. "Class, take your seats. Latwanda, see to the homework. Then go to my Out basket and pass back the papers there. The rest of you, get ready for a spelling test."

Toni scanned the room. Susan's name for plant waterer had been replaced with Mattie's.

Her silhouette must be up, thought Toni, hunting for Susan's paper silhouette on the back wall. *Two down from mine.* That space was empty, too. Every sign that Susan Lawrence had been a student in Room 308 was gone.

Mrs. Swallow directed the children involved in the quarrel outside the room. Toni trailed at the end, her eyes registering every empty place that had once contained some vestige of Susan Lawrence.

"Where are Susan's things?" demanded Toni, not addressing her teacher by name. "Why isn't her name on her coat hook? Who took her things? Who took down her silhouette?"

"Antoinette Douglas, calm down. *I* removed Susan's name and belongings. Last night I took them to her family," said Mrs. Swallow. "How can you accuse your classmates of stealing from Susan? You know we don't steal in our room."

"But why? Why? Why did you take her stuff away? Why did you do that?" Toni repeated, resisting the pressure of Mattie's hand on her arm. She ignored Raymond's warning look.

The children were stunned. No one had ever raised their voice to Mrs. Swallow.

"Children, go inside and study. Toni, you stay here."

"Toni, try to hold your temper," Raymond said.

Mattie touched Toni, her face pleading. Toni clenched her hands at her sides. She hated Mrs. Swallow, hated her for being able to erase Susan like that, hated her for staring down at her with those sorrowful eyes, hated her for accepting that her friend Susan Lawrence was really gone and would never again sit at the desk by the coleus and ivy plants.

"Oh, Toni," began the teacher.

Toni tightened inside. Every grown-up she knew started their sentences with the same sorry "Oh, Toni." She didn't want to hear it any more. She wanted to hear Susan's "Hi, girl!"

"Oh, Toni, I can't tell you how sorry, how shocked and unhappy I am that Susan was killed. I am aware that you two were very close," Mrs. Swallow said. "I know that you're upset, but I did what I believe is best. For everyone. Especially you."

"But why so fast? Why did you get rid of everything?

Why?" she hollered, glaring at her teacher. "You had no right! You didn't even know her. You're not our regular teacher. You're just a substitute!"

Abruptly Toni darted into the room and grabbed her jacket. Past Mrs. Swallow, down the hall, down the stairs, past the hall monitors, and out the main door she raced. The cold wind cut through her wool slacks and sweater like a scythe. She slowed down and put on her jacket.

The office would call her parents.

Shh—shoot, now I'm in trouble.

She decided to find an empty vestibule to rest in. On that block were large apartment buildings. Toni chose one randomly and plopped down on the vestibule stairs.

Where can I go now? she thought.

Home was out. So was school. Toni rummaged in her jacket pockets. Anxiously she counted out two dollars in change, and she had stuffed a five-dollar bill in her back pocket that morning. It was more than enough for bus fare. But a bus to where?

Stepping out into the sharp air, Toni selected a shiny dime and flipped it in her hand. *Heads, walk right. Tails, go left.* The coin rotated. Toni began walking away from home and school.

Half a block later, Toni grabbed her neck. She had left her purse in school. The piece of orange yarn with the house keys was in it. She remembered stuffing the keys into her purse earlier that morning. What a dumb thing to do!

"Well, I'm not going back there to get it," she said out loud, turning down the street. She spotted a large park just ahead. With a destination in mind, running through red lights, she fled all the way to the park and fell onto the first empty bench.

A familiar voice called her name, but she was too exhausted to move. Raymond came jogging up. "Toni, I knew I'd find you by the park." Raymond collapsed on the same bench to catch his breath. "Come on back with me. I told Mrs. Swallow I'd get you." He zipped up his black and gray thermal jacket and dug for his gloves. "Where are your gloves?"

"I don't know," Toni said.

"Here, take mine. No use freezing to death."

"I'm never going back to that room again, Raymond." Toni stared at him. "Mrs. Swallow was wrong."

"I'm not sure, Toni. What good does it do to keep Susan's things? Anyway, Mrs. Swallow is the teacher. What do you want to do?" he asked.

"I want to catch a bus and ride a while."

"We should get back to school," he said. "But when you get that look, I can't change your mind. I'm coming with you."

Toni and Raymond caught the next bus and transferred, getting off three blocks from Lake Michigan. In the summer the streets were congested with people riding bicycles and pushing strollers. She and Susan had often biked over there. Sometimes Mattie had joined them.

They climbed the steps and crossed the pedestrian bridge that spanned the freeway. Ahead was her favorite place. Susan's, too. The lake was a dull gray. Waves, whipped by the wind, foamed and frothed a path to the shore, only to ebb and fall. The sun broke through. Bands of light streaked across the choppy surface of the water.

Raymond stood by the rocks, watching Toni. She knelt on the cold sand, clutching her jacket close. Lowering her head, she prayed. "Dear Jesus, please bring Susan back. I love her. Stop all this and make her alive again. Please. Amen."

Hoping for a miracle, Toni lifted her head, only to flinch at a blast of lake wind. Nothing had changed.

"You feel better?" Raymond asked when she walked over to him.

"Not much."

"Toni, you remember when Sam got sick? In third grade?" he asked as they trudged back to the bus stop.

Toni nodded. Sam had been Raymond's dog, a mutt. Sam had gotten so sick he couldn't see or walk.

"Look, I know that Sam was just a dog and Susan's a person, a girl, but you helped me take him to the vet to be put to sleep. I just wish I could help you now."

"Raymond, you know how you kept saying 'Why did this happen to Sam?' That's how I feel now. Why Susan? I'm here. Why isn't she here with me?" Toni began to cry.

"I don't know why bad things happen. Living in the projects, I've seen a lot of trouble."

"What do you do about it?" she asked.

"Help my family. Get into a good school like King. Buy my computer," he said. "And fight when I have to. Let's eat. I've got some money."

"No, you save your money, Raymond. I'll treat," Toni said. "And thanks for coming after me."

There was a deli by the bus stop. Raymond opened the door for Toni, and they went in. On top of the counter Toni saw a basket with sesame seed breadsticks. Impulsively she bought two packages. Then Toni and Raymond shared a sandwich and some potato chips and went outside to wait on the cold corner. The bus took a long time to come.

With a promise to Raymond to return to school after lunchtime, Toni got off at her stop and headed home. She rang Mrs. Stamps's bell and was relieved when her friend buzzed her in.

"Oh, Toni my dear, I'm happy to see you," said Mrs. Stamps, holding Hannibal back. "I've been so worried about you!"

"Can I come in for a while?"

"No, dear, you'd better go upstairs," Mrs. Stamps said. "Your mother stopped by here looking for you not long ago. She's very upset. Hurry on, now."

Left alone on the dim landing, Toni peered at the brown carpeted steps that ended in front of her apartment. In a matter of days, her world had changed to a place where she felt lost and unhappy. Just two days. Each footstep she took weighed a ton.

"Toni! Where in the world have you been? Get yourself in here right now! I want an explanation, and I want one now!"

Toni opened her mouth, but her mother kept ranting.

"Running away from school! Your father is ready to call the police! Mrs. Reynolds calling me in the middle of the day!" she continued, slamming the door behind Toni. "Hollering and talking back to your teacher! Yes, I know about that. Screaming and calling the children dirty thieves!"

"But you don't know my side, Mama," Toni said. "Mrs. Swallow took all of Susan's stuff! She just erased Susan. Threw away her name card and everything!"

The telephone rang. Giving Toni a look that meant she wasn't finished with her, Mrs. Douglas hurried to answer it.

"She's home, Harold. . . . Yes, she's just fine. . . . I don't know yet. . . . No, don't come home. I can handle this. . . . Let's wait until tonight. . . . Yes, fine." Slowly Mrs. Douglas replaced the receiver.

"Now, where have you been?"

"I rode the bus to the lake. Raymond came with me," said Toni. "We just walked around. Then we caught the bus home. That teacher didn't have to touch Susan's stuff, Mama. I could have taken it to Mother Dear. Mrs. Swallow is just a sub. I'm Susan's friend."

Mrs. Douglas composed herself and stared at her daughter for a long moment.

"Thank heaven Raymond was with you. He has more sense than you do right now. I'm just upset. I know this is a rough time for you, Toni. You loved Susan, and I know this hurts you—but Susan is dead." She emphasized the last three words. "Keeping those things around won't change that. Believe me, I know and so does your teacher." Mrs. Douglas's slim body stiffened, as if some forgotten upset had surfaced.

Toni stood there. What could she say?

"I'm sorry for getting so mad. I was terrified that something had happened to you," Mrs. Douglas said. "Let's have some lunch together. Then you're going back to school."

All the kids in Room 308 gaped at Toni that afternoon. The only way to escape their stares was to bury her head in the first book she could snatch out of her desk. Mattie touched her shoulder.

"Where did you go?" she asked.

"Away from this room," Toni said.

Toni waited for Mrs. Swallow to do something to her. But her teacher said nothing.

In the middle of a spelling test, a messenger came in and handed the teacher a note. With a quick word to Mattie to finish giving the exam, she left the room.

When Mrs. Swallow returned, Toni jumped.

"Class, give me your attention," Mrs. Swallow said. "Susan Lawrence's grandparents have asked our class to come to the wake and the funeral."

The children looked surprised and whispered to one another.

Mrs. Swallow focused her attention on Toni. "We will be a part of the funeral service. This is an honor."

Stressing that only children with written parental permission would be allowed to attend, the teacher began writing on the front blackboard. Toni watched as she filled the space with her large, clear script. Her classmates, including Mattie, took out their pencils and copied the form. They all agreed to bring it back, signed, the next day. Mrs. Swallow repeated that no one had to attend, but that it would be a way to show their friendship with Susan and sympathy for her family. Toni heard her tell them to think about an appropriate song and poem.

"Now, all late homework is due tomorrow! The committees for our Christmas party will meet during morning recess, and we'll vote on a program," she concluded.

The bell rang. Toni tried to forget the name of the funeral home, the date, time, and place for the wake and funeral services. Mattie lined up next to her.

"Toni, I have to go to the dentist with Matt," she said as they went down the stairs. "But I'll call you tonight, okay? Here." She handed Toni a piece of notebook paper. "I copied the permission slip down for you."

Dumbly Toni accepted it. Mattie gave her a quick

kiss on the cheek and took off.

When Carl saw his sister, he exploded, running up and hugging her. "Toni! Toni!"

"Come on, Carl, stop that!" She pushed him away.

Carl whimpered, and fat tears slid down his cheeks. "Don't you be mean to me!" he said.

Toni released a long breath. He could be so sensitive. "Oh, Carl, I'm not being mean to you. I'm sorry. Don't cry," she said, bending down to embrace him.

He sobbed harder. Puzzled, Toni carefully removed his streaked glasses and put them in her pocket.

"Hey, come on, Carl. What's the matter?" Toni hunted for a tissue to wipe his nose. He was such a messy crier.

"Toni, is a car going to make you die? Like Susie?"

"Where did you get that crazy idea from?"

"Is it? Is it?" he asked, snatching at her jacket.

She wiped his snotty nose with her glove. "No, kid, not me. I promise to be extra careful. Dig in one of those condemned pockets of yours and find a lemon drop for us."

"Toni, how do you know?"

Exasperated, Toni answered, "Because I know, Carl. If I say I know, then I know."

He was quiet for the next twenty feet. He handed her a piece of candy, blowing at the lint.

"Why didn't Susie know?"

"Oh, Carl," said Toni through clenched teeth. "Here, take my hand." They stepped off a curb.

"Where's Susie gone to? Daddy told me she was gone. Can you and me go see her? Can we, Toni?"

"Carl Andrew Douglas," she warned.

"I want to see Susie. I miss her."

"Carl, I don't know where she is."

"Do Daddy and Mama know?"

She started to cry.

"Please don't cry, Toni. Here." He reached into his mouth and offered his candy, the last one.

"I do know where Susan is, Carl," she admitted.

"Can we go see her?"

The permission form in her pocket said that Susan was at Foster's Funeral Home, visiting hours from 9 A.M. to 9 P.M. The wake was two days from then, on Saturday. On Sunday, at 10 A.M., the funeral services would be held. Instead of answering her brother, Toni took his small hand and started walking home.

Later that afternoon Toni forced herself to work on the homework she'd missed. In a way, it was a relief to do something besides think about Susan. The room was quiet except for the sound of her music box.

When Mattie called, they talked briefly because Mattie's mouth was sore from three fillings. And as soon as she hung up, she found her brother standing before her.

"Toni?"

"What is it?"

"When do we go see Susie?"

"I don't know. Anyway, you're too young to go."

"Nope. Jon Ella and Harry Edwards are younger

than me and they went to see their auntie dead. They told me. So there."

Toni shook her head. With his tongue wedged in his left cheek, Carl looked as if he meant business.

"Carl, you do what I say or else."

"No, no, no, no." He stomped. "No, no, no."

"All right, if I go, you go," Toni said, knowing he wouldn't stop until she did.

"Stick out your thumb," he ordered.

"Ah, Carl, can't you take my word?" Seeing the refusal on his face, she complied. They put their thumbs together and twisted them, sealing the agreement.

"I'm hungry. I can't reach the ketchup," he said, grinning now. Together they went to the kitchen.

Toni was still doing schoolwork when her parents came home. They looked in, then closed her door. She was relieved to be left alone in her room.

Dinner was good. Daddy had brought home pizza and salad. Toni discovered that she was starving as she bit into chunks of mushroom, sausage, pepperoni, and green onion.

"There's something that we need to discuss." Her father sat next to her, wiping some pizza sauce off his moustache. "Susan's wake is Saturday, and the funeral is Sunday."

"I don't want to go," she heard herself sputter. "Not to the wake. Not to the funeral."

"Honey, I know you haven't been to a funeral before, but Susan was your friend," her mother said.

"Harold, maybe we should talk about this later."

"No, Dot, I want this funeral business cleared up before it gets out of hand. Toni, your mother and I want you to be there. Carl, too."

"Mama, can I watch TV?" squeaked Carl, sneaking a piece of pizza into his napkin.

"No, son, you stay here," said Mr. Douglas, returning the pizza to Carl's plate.

Carl sucked his thumb and pulled his right earlobe. Toni's mother lifted him to her lap.

Toni sat there. Her hands twisted around each other.

"Pumpkin, it is very hard to see a person you have loved dead, but funerals are a way for families and friends to say—" He hesitated.

"A way to say good-bye. Going to the wake and the funeral makes you face up and begin to let go," continued Mrs. Douglas, her voice like mist. "Like burying Mabel. Lord knows, I didn't want to see my baby sister in a coffin. It hurt, Toni. But I had to go, to be there with her." Toni saw her mother's hands clasp Carl closer, making him squirm.

"I'm scared to see Susan," Toni said. "I don't want to see her dead."

"That's normal, honey. But staying home won't make you less afraid."

"I want you to think about what we've said, Pumpkin." Her father hugged her.

"And think about Mother Dear and Father Lawrence, what a terrible time this is for them," Mrs.

Douglas added as she got up to put Carl to bed.

In bed, what Toni thought was that she'd had enough talks and death and feeling sad. The events of the past two days were rubbing her raw. There was no way to make Saturday and Sunday vanish. She buried her head under her pillow and finally fell asleep.

Sometime during the night, she woke up, sweaty and sticky. She tiptoed to the bathroom. She was bleeding a little. Her second period. Startled, Toni went through the still unfamiliar ritual of cleaning herself and pressing a napkin to a clean pair of panties.

Not long after she had climbed under the covers, Toni heard Carl's small padded feet hit the floor as he headed for the bathroom. She sat up to wait. Sometimes he tripped and got scared.

"Toni. Button me up. Too tired," he said, stopping in her open doorway with his giraffe in hand.

"Okay. You want to sleep with me?" Toni's invitation surprised her.

"You bet!"

"Climb in carefully. Put your pet on the other side," she ordered, smiling in spite of herself. Her body relaxed.

"Toni? You sleep?" came his voice.

"Almost, and you should be, too."

"Remember, you promised me to go see Susie," he said, drifting back to sleep.

"I remember, Carl," Toni said. "A promise is a promise."

6

Unequal Parts

Carl's snores woke Toni. She rolled over carefully, then got up and went to the bathroom. Her inspection revealed only a small amount of bleeding. And she had no cramps. *I hope having a period stays like this,* she thought.

Despite Mama's talks about what starting a menstrual cycle meant and the books and diagrams, the actual experience unnerved her. Toni knew that what was happening to her body was normal. Yet this stage of growing up didn't feel like losing her baby teeth or gaining an inch in height. This time she felt as if another person were growing out of her, replacing her, making her once-predictable body something to be watched. There was no telling what might happen next.

Toni dressed in a pair of new jeans, red-and-white-striped leg warmers, and her western blouse and vest. She gathered her books and went to the kitchen table to complete her homework. As she wrote the last spelling sentence, she heard her parents stirring. Toni sighed. Keeping her promise to Carl meant taking action today. She might need Mattie's help.

Mattie wasn't at the mailbox. Toni waited, stamping her feet in the cold to keep warm, but Mattie didn't show up. After she dropped Carl off, she spied her friend.

"I waited for you. What happened?" Toni asked, her breath spiralling like smoke in the winter air.

"I overslept." Mattie's face looked drawn and tired.

"You feel all right?" asked Toni.

"Not really." Mattie gazed away. "Mama had a bad night, and with what happened to Susan, I'm tired."

"Look, there's something I want to do after school. I need you to help me. Will you?" Toni pleaded.

"What is it?"

"Do you have to baby-sit?"

"First you tell me what you need help with," said Mattie, one gloved hand on her hip.

"I need you to go with me and Carl to Foster's Funeral Home," Toni said. "I have to go and see Susan. See her for myself. Today, after school, before the wake tomorrow."

Mattie looked at Toni. Her angular face was still and void of expression.

"That's where my father was. At Foster's," Mattie said softly. "Okay, Toni."

Toni sighed. "Thanks, Mattie. Will they let us see her?"

"I think so. You got bus fare? We have to transfer."

"Yes, I took money out of my drawer this morning."

For part of the morning, Toni fought to control her feelings about Susan's death. The Christmas committees met to discuss the party. Kids argued about refreshments, records, and games. Should they have punch with or without ginger ale? Should the games or the dancing come first?

Suddenly Toni grabbed the wooden bathroom pass. Her teacher nodded permission. All the grieving gathered inside her like a storm cloud. She had to run away, away from kids planning for a party that Susan wouldn't be able to enjoy.

Dummies! Dummies who don't care! Sitting there talking about punch and cake and who's going to wear what. They're crazy! Toni shoved the bathroom door open. Plastic mirrors threw back her face, distorting her features.

Toni locked one of the stall doors and sat down. Often the bathroom had served as her alone place, even at school. Sometimes being by herself was a comfort. But today thoughts of Susan's death prevented the relief she sought.

The bathroom door banged open.

"Toni? You in here?"

"What do you want?" Toni opened the door and walked out.

"Mrs. Swallow sent me to get you," Mattie explained. "What's wrong?"

Gazing at her friend, Toni wondered if she would understand. *Mattie can be such a "mighty battlemaid" sometimes. She might get mad at me,* Toni thought. *But who else my age can I talk to?* Swallowing her doubts, Toni came to a decision.

"Mattie, when your father passed away, did people just go on? I mean, did they act like nothing had happened?"

Mattie leaned against the sink by the door. "I came to school and the kids were jumping double dutch, talking about parties. Yeah, even you. You were all happy about some special slumber party at Susan's that weekend. You got mad at me because I wouldn't come."

"I'm sorry, Mattie. I didn't know." Toni's voice was subdued.

"Neither did I." She sighed. "I never had anybody I loved die. I still miss him."

"What do you do about it?"

"Cry," Mattie admitted. "And work as hard as I can to make him proud of me. We'd better get back to the room."

Mrs. Swallow called Toni up to her desk when she returned.

"Are you all right?" she asked quietly.

"Yes, Mrs. Swallow."

"I know that this is a difficult time for you, Toni.

Is there anything I can do to help you?" She paused.
"If you need to talk, just tell me. Maybe work will
make this time easier for you. I'm going to start giving
you five word problems twice a week. Regular practice
will help you learn faster." Mrs. Swallow handed Toni
a dittoed sheet of problems.

Toni took them and sat down.

Mrs. Swallow got up and called for attention. The
Christmas tree earrings whirled around.

"I read your suggestions and have put together a
program for our part in Susan's funeral. We don't have
much time, so I expect your full cooperation." She
paused, her eyes sweeping the room.

Toni squirmed and reached for a pencil to doodle
with. There was so much to concentrate on—the
scratches on her desk top, the pictures in her head,
the figures she could draw. The activity around her
became a blur.

"Toni, you're supposed to join my group," said a
quiet, insistent voice.

"Huh? What?"

"You're in my group. Over here."

"Group for what?"

"To practice the song for the funeral service. You
don't have to say anything. Just sit close to me. I won't
let anybody bother you."

Mattie was an efficient organizer. There would be a
poem read by Raymond. Mattie would sing a solo with
the church choir. And the class would sing near the

end of the service. The program was only for the funeral. Nothing but their presence would be expected at the wake.

Numb, Toni endured the discussion, welcoming Mattie's occasional touch. Mechanically she lined up with her class and practiced the song.

After school Toni and Mattie went to get Carl. "What did you tell your parents about being late today?" said Mattie.

"Uh, nothing."

"Well, what are you going to tell them? We'll need about twenty minutes or more to get there, the same time to get back, plus the length of time we're there. That's at least an hour," she calculated.

"I'll make up something," Toni said. "Mattie, do you think I should go ahead with this?"

Before Mattie could answer, Carl ran up. He was a showstopper in his red snowsuit and the green wool hat Toni had crocheted for him last Christmas to match his scarf. She checked to make sure that his mittens were pinned to his sleeves. They were.

Worried, she turned her attention to Mattie, who was studiously buttoning her brown jacket over two black sweaters. She pulled a limp lavender scarf out of her pocket and fastened it around her neck.

"Do you need to do this? I can't tell you if this is right or wrong." Mattie picked up her books. "When my daddy died, I did some weird things."

"Like what?"

"I don't want to talk about it now," Mattie said.

"Toni! Toni! Push me in the swing!" Her brother hurtled recklessly around her, a red roller coaster in motion.

"No time for swinging and playing now. Carl, remember that promise I made last night? Well. . . ." Then Toni made her decision. "Mattie is going with us to see Susan. We have to hurry."

Toni stared out the grimy bus window. It wasn't fair for Susan to go and leave her like that! Why couldn't she have been more careful? Looked both ways before she crossed the street?

A horrifying thought occurred to Toni. What would a dead Susan look like? Conjuring up an image of Susan dead was impossible. Susan had never been still. Memories of Susan laughing and yelling flitted before her. Susan running to catch the bus in front of the Art Institute, pretending to be an international spy in a trenchcoat and sunglasses! Susan eating two oatmeal cookies at the same time. Susan stumbling in those silly high heels on Halloween. Susan alive.

"We get off at the next stop," said Mattie, jolting Toni back to the present. "You sure you want to do this? We'll go to the wake tomorrow."

Toni nodded. "I don't want to see her for the first time with all those people around," she explained.

"Then let's go." There was a grim edge to Mattie's voice as she guided Carl off the bus. Ahead loomed Foster's Funeral Home.

"Uh, Mattie, did you ever see somebody young like us dead?" Toni asked.

"No, just my daddy."

"I know," Carl said. "They look asleep. That's what Jon Ella and Harry Edwards told me. Dead people go to sleep and then the boogeyman brings them bologna sandwiches with mayonnaise and lots of ketchup. As much ketchup as they want," he repeated. "And all the chocolate cake they want, too!"

Toni ignored him.

"How did your father look, Mattie?"

"Just like Carl said, like he was asleep, but real straight and stiff, too. His face looked like there was powder on it."

"What do you think Susan's going to look like?" Her voice quaked.

"Like she's dead."

Seeing Toni's expression, Mattie added, "I'm sorry, Toni. I'm scared, too."

"You are? I'm so afraid," Toni admitted. "Do you think she'll have her braces on?"

Mattie shrugged.

Then Toni saw the funeral home. A dark-green canopy stretched from the front door to the sidewalk. The clean brick building had several large windows. Toni wondered why the drapes were closed in the afternoon. What was there to hide?

Mattie walked up and pushed at the front door. Nothing happened. Laughing nervously, she rang a small black bell to the right of the door. They heard a chime sound. Mattie pressed the bell again.

A tall, brown-skinned woman appeared. She moved aside to let the shivering kids in.

"Good afternoon. I'm Mrs. Mack, the receptionist. And you're . . ."

"I'm Carl Andrew Douglas," said Carl, struggling to pull off the mittens that were pinned to his sleeves.

The woman smiled.

"I'm Toni Douglas and this is my friend, Mattie Benson," said Toni, remembering her manners.

"Mattie Benson. . . ." Mrs. Mack thought for a moment. "Oh, yes, how are you, Mattie, and your mother and brother?"

"You remember us?" said Mattie.

"Of course I do. Is everyone fine?"

Mattie said yes.

"Now, how may I help you?"

"Well—we—I wanted to see my friend. Our teacher said she was here," stammered Toni. "Her name is Susan, Susan Lawrence."

"Oh, yes. This is somewhat unusual. Sit down a minute while I get the telephone. I won't be long."

Mrs. Mack's modulated tones complemented the decor of the room. Toni glanced about, expecting to see dead bodies jump out at her. Wood paneling covered one wall, and silky beige wallpaper adorned the others. She resisted the urge to reach out and rub it. Everything in the room blended into a soft beige: the carpet under her feet, the chair that Carl was swinging his legs from, the sofa, and the drapes.

Wonder how they got all this to match the wallpaper, Toni thought. She walked over to Mattie, who was reading something on a wooden stand that stood before a long, empty hall. Toni peered over her shoulder at the notice in neat white block letters: Slumber Room— Mrs. Claudia Mae Scott; Pending—Mr. James Robinson; Chapel of Peace—Miss Susan Denise Lawrence. Goose pimples broke out all over Toni's arms. She jumped when Mrs. Mack came up behind her.

"Can we see Susan now?" asked Mattie.

"Well, you can if you want to. It's not against the rules. But I would certainly feel better if your parents were here with you, or some responsible adult." Mrs. Mack sounded as if she were reciting a speech. "Do your parents know that you three are here?"

Before they could respond, Carl tugged at Toni. "I'm hungry. Are we going to eat? Where's Susie?"

"Let's sit down." Mrs. Mack gestured at the sofa.

Torn between walking down that hall, into the Chapel of Peace, or out the front door, Toni stood where she was.

"I can tell that you're not too sure about this. I can certainly understand your feelings. Why not think this over and talk to your family?" Mrs. Mack said. "The wake for your friend is tomorrow. Certainly you can see her then."

"Toni?" asked Mattie.

"I'm hungry, Toni. I have to go to the bathroom, now," repeated Carl.

Toni wrestled with her feelings. *One thing is certain. Susan is here. Her name on the stand says so. So does this lady. No, I don't want to see Susan, not now, not here!* Toni shook her head and ran outside, leaving Mattie to take Carl to the bathroom.

The bus ride home was quiet. Toni and Mattie parted at the corner.

"See you tomorrow at the wake?"

"I don't know, Mattie. Thanks for going with me," replied Toni, bowing her bare head against the wind. With Carl complaining all the way, she hurried to beat her parents home.

They bumped into Mrs. Stamps and Hannibal in the vestibule.

"Oh, Toni my dear and Carl darling, I'm so glad to see you two." She beamed. "How are you doing, my dear? Now, don't say fine. No one can be doing fine when they lose someone they love."

"We went to the funeral place where Susie is sleeping," said Carl.

"Oh, did you?" Mrs. Stamps's eyebrows lifted an inch.

"But we didn't get to see Susie," said Carl. "She's asleep right now. I'm hungry, Nana."

"I bet you are, Carl. Come on in and have something to eat while Toni leaves a note for your parents."

By the time Toni rejoined them, Mrs. Stamps had

Carl happily munching on a cheese sandwich and drinking milk. Hannibal lounged in the corner. The kitchen resembled a hothouse, with plants hanging from the ceiling. Trails of leafy vines dangled down the walls. The sounds of the hissing radiator and the calypso song on the radio made death seem unreal. Toni sank into a kitchen chair.

"Carl, watch your frog mug. Look at what you're doing," Mrs. Stamps said as she poured peppermint tea from a blue teapot with a dragon-head spout.

"I've been worried about you, my dear." She shook her head from side to side twice. "With Susan gone and all. So tragic, so needless. And her poor family."

"How are they?" Toni hadn't thought much about them.

"Susan's grandparents are not doing well. Mother Dear is confined to her bed. Susan's father is trying to hold things together. The mother barely talks and is absolutely no help to anyone. Poor Father Lawrence, he looks as though he's aged fifty years! They need our prayers."

Tears spilled from Toni's eyes. "I miss Susan so much. Nothing is going right."

"Cry, child. Here, use this." And she handed Toni a lace handkerchief that smelled of rose petals. "Take a sip of tea. Try that cake with the coconut icing."

"Tomorrow's the wake and then the funeral is on Sunday. I'm supposed to go, but I don't want to," Toni said, blowing her sore nose.

"I see."

"Are you going, Mrs. Stamps?"

"Of course I am; it's my duty. The Lawrences are members of our church family, and they're my personal friends," she said, watching Toni's face. "I don't look forward to the wake and the funeral. But I'd never let my friends grieve alone."

After more tea and cake, Toni and her brother walked the one flight up. The concentration she needed to solve the word problems was missing, so she joined Carl and turned the television set up so she could hear. When Toni heard her parents come in, she and Carl both ran to the door.

Toni's father was carrying a huge green tree with cones. Carl jumped with glee. Toni was shocked. *Tonight? Why did he get a Christmas tree tonight?* Toni thought. She watched as her mother got the stand and the two of them positioned the tree.

"Toni, stand back and tell me if the tree is straight," her father said.

Instead she rushed to her room and closed the door. *They don't care about Susan. How can they think about Christmas?*

"Toni, what's wrong?" Her mother stood by her bed.

"How could Daddy bring home a tree today?"

"Oh, honey. Christmas is one of the worst times for a wake and a funeral. But, believe me, there's no such thing as a good time for any of this." Mrs. Douglas smoothed Toni's hair.

"I don't feel good," Toni mumbled, staring angrily at the wall. "I hate Christmas; it's for babies!"

"No, you don't," her mother said. "What you hate is what happened to Susan, and so do we all."

Toni turned away from her mother. With a sigh, Mrs. Douglas left and closed the door behind her.

After dinner Toni put on her coat, gloves, and boots. She carried the garbage down the back steps to the big can. The latest snowfall had been heavy. The top layer was already frozen and crunched beneath her boots. Standing in the snow and shivering, Toni scanned the dark sky. On an invisible thread, the moon hung, a sliver of pale light, without warmth.

7

Multiplying the Distance

It was "wake day." As comforting as staying under the covers was, Toni knew that she had to get up. She washed up and put on her robe. As she tugged the belt tighter, she noticed the fragrance of the Christmas tree. In a way Toni regretted not joining her family last night to decorate the tree. She'd heard them laughing and fussing together. A larger part of her yearned to burrow into a hole and hide out all weekend. Footsteps sounded behind her.

"No moping today, Toni. We're going to do some housecleaning, then head for the shopping center," Mrs. Douglas said. "Just you and me. We'll stop for lunch. Believe me, the day will go a lot faster if you stay busy."

Her mother's advice turned out to be right. The two of them moved quickly from task to task, pausing only for a cup of soup and a sandwich. And when the family sat down for dinner, Toni was amazed at the hour. The day had ended.

Nothing could hold back the anxiety and sadness Toni felt as her family walked up the steps to the Lawrences' home. They would be riding with Susan's family to the funeral home for the wake.

Susan's father greeted them at the door. He was almost as tall as Toni's father but had a full Afro and no moustache. He led them to the living room. Father Lawrence and Mother Dear were waiting for them. Toni swallowed hard when she saw the change in them. There had been no exaggeration in Mrs. Stamps's description.

When the limousine parked in front of Foster's Funeral Home, Toni's stomach churned. She nodded at Mrs. Mack and went over to the stand, where she read "Quiet Hour, 7–8 P.M., Susan Denise Lawrence, Chapel of Peace."

The Reverend Webster was greeting the Lawrences. His portly, solemn dignity was deceptive. Those church members who attended his fiery Sunday sermons could testify that at times he made them feel the fires of hell or hear the harps of heaven.

Down that hallway is the Chapel of Peace, thought Toni. *And in there, Susan.* Her parents took her hand as they followed the bereaved family and their minister into the chapel. Toni saw a blur of wood, rock, and glass. The vaulted ceiling soared above them.

Toni gasped. Rough rock covered the front wall, forming a huge inverted V that ended at the ceiling. Lush baskets of flowers hung from hooks scattered among chunks of the multicolored rocks. There were roses in pink, yellow, white, and red, carnations, gladiolas, daisies, and baby's breath. Toni tried to see if there were any lilies, recalling Susan's delight when she discovered that her name meant "lily." But she couldn't find any. Beneath all that splendor, in a circle of wreaths, stood a small casket. Toni averted her eyes.

As they got closer and closer to the casket, Toni's breath quickened.

The minister entered a special room to the right of the casket, where the immediate family could sit. Was that where they had to go? The room was separated from the casket by a large window.

"No, no, I won't sit in there," Mother Dear protested. "I want to be near my grandbaby."

"But, Mother, I thought that some privacy would help you calm down." Father Lawrence patted her hand.

"No, I can't be in there. I won't have a window between me and my grandbaby, please. I want to be out here with our friends."

For the first time, Toni paid attention to Susan's mother. She seemed so removed from everything. Like a sleepwalker.

Why did she come to Chicago for this? Toni thought. *Why didn't she come when Susan needed her?*

"All right, dear. Reverend Webster, the family will

sit in the first pew, close to Susan," said Father Lawrence, with nods of assent from his son.

Toni's knees buckled, then straightened. She had to look at her friend.

Susan hates pink! Don't they know that?

Dozens of pink and white carnations encircled the casket. A pink tufted satin interior surrounded Susan. *Susan is asleep. She's just asleep. In a minute she'll wake up, shake the sleep off, and laugh. Then we'll go home together and dump that pink dress,* thought Toni, staring at Susan.

Toni's thoughts shifted again. A new pink dress. Who had selected it? Susan's mother? Toni liked the tiny embroidered flowers and ruffles on the collar. The lower half of Susan's body was covered by the casket. A bed of flowers was draped over that part of the casket. Who had combed and brushed Susan's hair into two ponytails tied with pink satin ribbons?

In her hands Susan held a small gold cross. She lay on a plush light pink satin pillow. Toni wanted to touch the pillow. *I hope the pillow's soft. Susan hates hard pillows. They give her headaches.* Hesitantly Toni examined her friend's face. Susan's bright hazel eyes were shut. Long, thick brown lashes rested on her face. Her mouth was closed so Toni couldn't see if she had her braces on or not. She hoped so. Susan was so proud of her braces! Susan looked like she was asleep. There were no signs of trauma. No scars. Nothing out of the ordinary. Except for the fact that Susan wasn't breathing.

Then Toni sat down. Carl was on one side of her, her mother on the other. The front pew was filled with Susan's family and the Douglases.

People began arriving. Toni saw the Bensons. Mattie smiled at her. Toni smiled back. There was Raymond, Ida, Latwanda, and, of course, her teacher. Mrs. Swallow stopped and talked to the Lawrences, touching Toni's cheek as she passed by. People were shaking their heads, crying, mumbling slow words to one another. There were even some white people, other than Mrs. Swallow. Probably people the Lawrences had worked with.

Then, as quietly as the wake had begun, it ended. The organ music stopped. The Chapel of Peace emptied. A man dressed in a dark blue suit came over and whispered to Father Lawrence and Susan's father. They stood up. Susan's mother bent her head. Mother Dear sobbed louder. "I can't leave my Susan. I can't leave my grandbaby. Oh! Dear Lord, help me bear this!" she cried. "Lord, why did you take her? Why? Why, Lord?"

Toni clutched Carl's hand, uncomfortable in the midst of so much emotion. The adults clustered around the old woman, supporting her, forcing her away from the casket, toward the door at the end of the aisle.

"What will we do? She's our grandbaby! She was so young, so young." Mother Lawrence turned back. "And she's all alone in there."

"Mother, we have to go. Our friends will be coming

to the house, you know that," said her son, his voice low. "Dr. Wilson said you have to rest. You gave him and Dad your word that you'd go right to bed after the wake."

"Please, Mother, our Susan's with God now. She'll never be alone," said the Reverend Webster. "Now you must rest."

But Toni couldn't stay in the hallway, mingling with the others. She ran back into the chapel one last time. She stood there, praying for a miracle. The only miracle was the pungent aroma of the flowers and the faint sound of water splashing. Dejected, she lifted her head and cautiously caressed Susan's face, flinching at the tight coolness. She wanted to kiss her friend, but she couldn't.

Toni had brought something special with her to leave with Susan. She took a package of breadsticks she had bought at the deli out of her purse and tucked them way under a fold in Susan's dress. Hearing her father call for her, Toni touched Susan's cheek for the last time.

The Lawrence home was packed with mourners. Toni drifted past the kitchen and dining room. Hams, turkeys, macaroni and cheese casseroles, rolls, cakes, pies, and more covered every surface. Mattie had told her that after the funeral it would happen all over again.

Gripping a plate of food, Toni escaped to the living room. She watched Carl devour a large piece of chocolate cake that he had probably charmed some unsuspecting woman into giving him. Her father was studying the crowd. Toni guessed that her mother was in the bedroom with Mother Dear. She saw people going to the door, barely knocking, and entering. The door to Susan's room was shut, too. *A house of closed doors,* Toni thought sadly.

Threading her way through muted conversations and past cups of coffee, tea, and punch, Toni crossed the living room to Susan's room. Stealthily easing the door open, she slid in. She could hear Mother Dear mourning through the walls.

The room hadn't changed much. Someone had neatly arranged Susan's collection of stuffed animals and dolls. Raggedy Ann grinned from her place in the center. Toni smiled. Susan had loved that old doll to wear and tear. One of her eyes was missing, and she was practically bald. Toni smoothed the places on her cloth body where Susan had attempted to repair the holes. *What's going to happen to all of this?* she wondered.

The door opened. "I figured you'd be in here. What are you doing?" Mattie closed the door.

"Just thinking. It was so noisy and crowded out there." Toni looked around. "Mattie, what did you do when you felt like this?"

"Cried. I did that a lot. I still do, on my birthday and different holidays." Mattie sighed. "So do my mother and Matt, though he'd never say so. I miss Daddy all the time."

"Who do you talk to?"

"Myself. I used to talk to Matt."

"Does your mother help you?"

Mattie looked weary. "Mama can hardly help herself. She's still in bad shape."

"What happened to your father's clothes?" asked Toni.

"Mama kept some and donated the rest to the church. Some she threw away."

"Oh."

The door opened again.

"Carl, what do you want?" Toni demanded.

"I found you!" Happy, he came in, closed the door, and plunked down next to his sister, his jaws working on a lemon drop.

"What do you want?"

"I saw a little boy on TV get hit by a car. He didn't die." Carl put his hand in Toni's.

"TV is TV, not real life. In real life sometimes you get saved and sometimes you don't. Now, no more questions, Carl."

"TV lies," Carl said, still sucking on his candy. "So the boogeyman came and took Susie with him, huh?"

"What in the world are you talking about now?" said Toni.

"Jon Ella and Harry Edwards told me that when people die—"

"I don't want to hear this!" said Toni.

"When people die, they get put in places called cemeteries, in big holes in the ground with their coats on to keep them warm, and the boogeyman comes every night to give them their sleepy medicine so they won't wake up in the dark and cry," Carl recited.

"Of all the crazy stories."

Mattie shook her head.

"Then the boogeyman gives them peanut butter and grape jelly sandwiches. And chocolate cake and chocolate-chip ice cream in the summer. Susie loves chocolate cake. I know," he concluded, looking superior.

"Carl, that's enough. I'm tired. Let's find Daddy and Mama," Toni said. Mattie nodded.

The crowd had thinned to a few close friends. The cuckoo clock above the piano in the living room sang out the late hour. There wasn't a sign of Christmas anywhere. Just used plates with scraps of food, empty, smudged glasses, and crumpled napkins.

"Kids, Dot, you ready to go? How's Mother Dear?" asked Toni's father.

Mrs. Douglas rubbed her forehead. "Oh, Harold, she finally dozed off. Father Lawrence is with her. I'm so worried. She might not be well enough to make it through the funeral. She's so determined to be there."

"We're giving Mattie, Matt, and Sheila a ride home," he said.

"Good," said Toni's mother, turning to hug Mattie's mom. "Sheila, you've helped all week. The others can clean up."

After kisses and hugs from Father Lawrence, Toni

climbed into the back seat next to Carl and Mattie and Matt. Their parents talked about the drunk driver.

"I heard Susan's father say that the guy who hit Susan was so drunk he fell down trying to walk a straight line," Mr. Douglas said. "He was crying about how sorry he was."

Toni cringed.

"And Susan was crossing with the light. I hope they put that jerk away for a long time," Mrs. Douglas added.

"How long can he get?" Toni asked.

Mrs. Benson turned around. "That depends on a lot of things. He could go to jail for three years. Or less."

"But he killed Susan! Three years isn't enough!" Toni cried, leaning forward.

"I agree."

"Toni, enough for tonight. You rest," her mother said, reaching around to push Toni back gently.

For Toni only seconds elapsed between the moment she leaned back, resting against Mattie, and the moment when her mother was helping her off with her coat and leading her to bed.

Recalling the breadsticks she had left with Susan in the Chapel of Peace, Toni twisted to one side and whispered, "Good night, Susan. Sleep tight. I love you."

8

No Remainder

Grown-ups are crazy! Why do they have funerals right after wakes? Toni wondered, exhausted. *One is enough. Two is too much.*

In the bathroom, fully dressed, Toni saw her reflection. That Sunday morning there were no excited twirls. The gray wool dress hung on her. She fingered the smocked bodice decorated with tiny pearl buttons. She had wanted to wear her pearl earrings, but her hands had picked up the Statue of Liberty earrings.

"These are the last things Susan gave me. But she stole them."

So instead of wearing the earrings, she wrapped them in a tissue and put them in her dress pocket. White nylon knee socks and leather ballerina shoes completed what she had selected to wear to the funeral.

Her brother fought wearing his clothes, driving Toni to the brink of anger. "Carl, you have to wear socks! Put on your Sunday shoes. No, not those gym shoes. You know better than that."

"These hard shoes hurt!" he said, peering under his bed for the mate to the gym shoe he was still holding.

"No, they don't hurt! You never said they hurt before. Get up from there right now. Hand me the pick and the brush."

Toni sat on the bed with Carl squeezed firmly between her legs. Combing his hair was always a battle.

"Don't ever think that I enjoy doing this, little brother. I'll be the happiest person in the world when you can do these things the right way all by yourself, believe me." Toni fussed, fluffing his hair with the pick, then brushing out the difficult tangles. "Why wasn't I lucky enough to be born the youngest? Then you'd have to take care of me. Don't move from this spot. I have to get the hair oil." Toni got up.

In the hall, Toni met her mother.

"You look so pretty," said Mrs. Douglas, who wore a black dress with a beige lace collar. "I want you to clear off the kitchen table. Make sure you put on an apron. I'll finish getting Carl ready."

"Thanks, Mama."

Frosty morning air hit the Douglas family. Silver clouds swelled over the horizon. The trees arched in icy grandeur, bearing the weight of snow and ice.

When they reached the Lawrences' building, they

saw the same black limousine that had taken them to the wake. But this time the driver took his grief-shocked, dry-eyed passengers to Ebenezer Baptist Church through brilliant morning sunshine.

Toni stared out of the window and lost herself in better times. Horse rides and fireworks. Fried chicken and potato salad picnics. Fights over whose turn it was to crank the ice-cream machine. She tasted cold watermelon on a humid August afternoon, juicy, sweet, and welcome. She saw Susan and Mattie competing to see who could spit the seeds the farthest, shouting that if they swallowed even one seed, it would start sprouting and send green shoots out their nose, ears, and mouth! All three of them hysterical with laughter, then soberly apologetic when Carl swallowed a seed and started to cry.

Happy families. Good times. Suddenly she shifted in her seat, feeling the flow from her period. Soon they'd get to church.

Black and purple banners were draped over the entrance to Ebenezer Baptist Church. Toni headed for the basement and the bathroom.

The noisy congestion of her church family was welcome after the lonely, silent limousine ride. Every choir was dressed—the Gospel Choir, the Adult Choir, and the Childrens' Choir. Mrs. Buchanan, the choir director, handed Toni her robe, light blue trimmed with gold braid.

At five minutes to ten, Mattie ran in, tearing off her

coat and offering excuses as she zipped up her robe. "Mom had trouble starting the car. I was afraid we would have to call a cab," Mattie said, smoothing the folds in her robe.

Toni was glad to see Mattie, knowing they'd sit together in the choir pews.

The organist played softly when the choirs marched in. As Toni kept time to the beat of the music, she started, remembering that this was her first funeral.

At least Mattie is a veteran! She knows what to do, thought Toni, seeing Susan before her.

"Oh, no!" she gasped. "Mattie, the top of the casket is closed! Susan can't breathe!"

Mattie stared at Toni in amazement. Then the irony of her words hit Toni. With visible effort, she folded her hands and stared beyond the closed casket.

The Reverend Webster slowly strode to his high chair before the congregation. An organ chord sounded. Father and Mother Lawrence came down the aisle, followed by Susan's father and mother. Walking erect, Father Lawrence supported his wife, who appeared ready to collapse on his arm. Toni couldn't see Mother Dear's face through the dark veil, but the white handkerchief in her gloved hand stood out, small and crushed.

The organ hushed. Toni bowed her head for the scripture and prayers. She studied the program. Susan's last school picture was on the front. Her mischievous grin clashed with the words below it: "In

Loving Remembrance of Susan Denise Lawrence."
Toni skipped past the birthdate and the month, day,
and year of her friend's death. The rest wasn't important, except for the word "interment," followed by
Willow Cemetery, Jackson, Mississippi.

Opening the program, Toni quickly scanned the inside pages. Her eyes strayed to the back of the program,
where the names of Susan's classmates were listed as
honorary pallbearers. Skimming the page for her
name, she was disappointed not to see some distinctive
notation, a star, signifying that her relationship with
Susan was special.

"Amen" and "Bless Jesus" closed the prayers. The
opening lines of "God's Tomorrow" sent a chill racing
down the sides of Toni's arms. The Reverend Webster's hearty baritone boomed, reverberating through
the pews. The organ began to rock, the music flew
higher and higher, sometimes leading the choirs, sometimes being led by them. Toni felt the sunlight on her
face. It illuminated each stained glass window that the
church had spent years raising money to buy. Too
choked to sing, Toni fingered the gold braid on her
robe.

"On behalf of the Lawrence family, Sister Douglas
will now come forward and acknowledge the many
expressions of sympathy offered for our daughter of
the church, Susan. Sister Douglas," called the minister, his black robes rippling like deep water in his
wake.

"Thank you, Reverend Webster, deacons, and

members of Ebenezer Baptist Church. On behalf of
the Lawrence family, I would like to thank you for
your kindnesses during this tragic time. . . ."

Toni breathed deeply. Her mother's calm, firm voice
muted the shock of seeing Susan locked up in a casket.
As she followed her mother's return to her seat, the
organist struck the series of chords for the Gospel
Choir. They sang the old music in the old ways. Turning around, Toni saw Mr. Captain in his regular place
near the rear of the choir and Mrs. Buchanan, who
commanded a well-deserved reputation for being able
to shout a hand-clapping solo. She listened as Mattie
sang the verse, and found the slow, steady cadence of
the spiritual soothing:

I do not know why art from me, my hopes are
    shattered.
God's perfect plan I cannot see.

Palms clapped in sharp, staccato slaps. Hands
pushed back the air and waved to testify agreement.
Nurses' aides in white uniforms, skilled in first aid,
readied themselves and scanned the pews. A young
mother screamed, "Jesus! Jesus! Help that baby!" She
writhed and twisted, caught up in the spirit of mourning that gripped the church family. Then another and
another keened as the Gospel Choir sang on:

Someday He'll make it plain to me
Someday when I His face shall see.

Down the center and side aisles, the nurses' aides marched swiftly, leading some wailers to a side room to recover. Uniformed ushers assisted them. Louder and louder the organ throbbed. Toni felt that her heart would burst from pain.

Choir voices merged with the shouts, screams, and moans of the church family, dipping deep into the well of ancient times and rhythms. The Gospel Choir was special. They sang the spirituals that had brought comfort to the miserable, freedom to the enslaved, and hope to the desperate for hundreds of years. Toni knew that to be a member of the Gospel Choir was an honor.

She dipped into that well with the rest of her church family, rocking and swaying to the music with Mattie, her hands and feet tapping the beat. Toni sang the words:

Someday from tears I shall be free
For someday I shall understand.

The organ died away. Raymond swallowed nervously as he came forward to read the class poem. The class had elected him to represent them. Everyone had worked hard on the poem. Toni watched Raymond take a breath and open the folder. He looked older to Toni in his navy suit and tie. She listened closely.

Susan was in our class
And her memory will always last.
She was a ray of sunshine

Taken from us before her time.
Sunshine Susan, we will miss you.

Your smile and your sparkle will live
In all our hearts and give
A special warmth and glow
Despite the tears that flow.
Sunshine Susan, we will miss you.
Sunshine Susan, we will miss you.

After the reading, Toni's class lined up on either side of Susan's casket. Mattie stepped forward to the microphone. Moments later Mattie's voice rang out the chorus, "Jesus wants me for a sunbeam." Her clear, high-spirited solo inspired Toni to join her choir. So Toni sang to Susan, making every muscle in her throat strain to deliver the words and the love in them. Then their part was over. The class, many in tears, took their seats.

The Reverend Webster began the sermon. His words drifted in and out.

What's he talking about? Something about a garden? Toni willed herself to concentrate.

"If we will but pause a moment and think on God's sweet heaven, pause a moment and remember that even God needs flowers for His garden. Lovely, innocent flowers that bloom in the sun and represent all that is good, all that is beautiful, all that is precious to us and to Him. These flowers are our children, the gift that we are sometimes called upon by our Savior, who sacrificed His only Son for us, the gift that only He may ask us to share with Him. Jesus is saying 'I need a beautiful flower for My garden. Let Me share your Susan.' "

The Reverend Webster was almost finished. Toni listened, struggling to make sense of his explanation for Susan's death.

"He will make it plain. Someday, with His grace and His love, we will understand, and our memories of Susan will be filled with a wondrous joy far greater than the regret and grief we share today, because Susan was always His first, and He shared that precious flower of a child with us for a while. To the Lawrence family I offer faith, the love and the comfort of our church and of our Shepherd."

Barely hearing the closing prayer, Toni slumped back. Music followed the family as they made their way to the casket and then down the aisle. The church was slow to empty. Toni gazed about her. *What Reverend Webster said isn't true. Susan isn't any flower in some garden. She's my friend.*

"Toni?" said Mattie.

"No," Toni said. "Susan is in that casket. I don't want to leave her here."

Members of the choirs filed out, leaving Toni there with Mattie.

"You ready?" Mattie asked. "Everybody is leaving."

"No, I won't go."

Carl ran up to her.

"Come on, now, we have to go," he said, taking her hand.

Toni stood, her knees shaking. This was it. After this, Susan would be taken away to be buried in Jackson, Mississippi, a city she'd never seen.

"I can't even go visit her grave." She looked back several times. The casket looked so lonely and small.

"I hope it's nice in Jackson, and warm," Toni confided to Mattie as they exchanged their robes for winter coats and hats.

"It is. Real warm and pretty," Mattie said.

"That's right, I forgot. You have family there."

Toni wanted to go home, but that wasn't possible. She had to accompany the rest of her family to the Lawrences' home for the after-funeral gathering.

It was more of last night. More food. More grown-ups talking angrily about the way Susan had been killed. More tears. More tension.

"Toni, Mother Dear wants to see you," said Mrs. Douglas. "Now, don't upset her. The shock of Susan's death could kill her. So just listen quietly to whatever she has to say."

Frightened, Toni obeyed. The bedroom was dimly lit. Mother Dear sat up in the middle of the big bed, still dressed, with a multicolored quilt over her. On the bedside table lay a plate of untouched food, a glass of water, and several bottles of pills.

"Mother Dear, here's Toni," said her mother, closing the door behind them.

"Yes, Toni, come here." Mother Dear's voice quivered.

Toni went over and kissed her cheek.

"Dot, where is it?" she asked, peering around the room.

"What, Mother Dear?"

"What I had sorted out to give Toni. I can't recall where I placed that bag." She frowned.

"I know what you mean. I'll get it. You just rest now." And Toni's mother left the room.

"Listen, Toni, Father Lawrence and I have to go home for a while. We have to take our Susie back home. I don't know when we'll—" She broke off, forgetting her place. "When I get back, I'll get everything in order. My poor son. I even feel sorry for my grand-baby's mother."

Toni's mother returned. She had a bag in her hand. Mother Dear reached out a shaky hand and took the bag, holding it with care.

"Toni, I want you to have these." She held tightly to them. "Now, before we leave for Jackson."

"I can't, I just can't," Toni said, afraid and mesmerized by the bag.

"Yes, you must," said the old woman with a hint of her former strength. "Toni, Susie loved you, and I won't have you going home with nothing to remember her by." She sighed, collapsing on the pillows. "Open it."

Toni's mother nodded to her to comply.

Toni hesitated, her heart pounding. She opened the bag and examined the contents. There were two photos of Susan, a gold chain necklace, the stuffed Teddy bear that usually sat next to Raggedy Ann, and a box of yellow stationery. Hot tears spilled from Toni's eyes, smudging the babyish blue glasses again and sliding across the plastic that covered the box of stationery. She thanked Mother Dear and repacked the odd assortment of gifts.

All her worries about King Academy—about entrance exams and word problems—seemed far away. Toni left, clutching a bag that threatened to drag her down.

Is this it? she cried inside. *Is this what happens when you die? Do you end up in a closed casket? Do the people you love hold on to you with stuff in a paper bag?* There were no answers anymore, just questions that hurt.

9

Unknown Quantities

"**H**oney, I have to meet with a graduate student after work," Mrs. Douglas said over her third cup of coffee. "Heat the meat loaf and rice. Oh! Fix a salad, too. You and Carl go ahead and eat. Your father and I have some last-minute Christmas shopping to do."

Toni stacked the breakfast dishes in the sink. She'd wash them after school.

Five days had gone by since Susan's funeral. Today was the last school day before the Christmas holiday. Today was also Friday, the day of the Christmas party. She had to hand in five word problems. Toni let out a deep breath.

"Mama, don't forget my Christmas list," said Carl, hopping out of his chair to grab his mother's arm. "You promised to remind Santa Claus."

"Carl, how could Santa possibly forget any of the twenty-seven items on your list?" She laughed, rumpling his hair. "Oh, Toni, what about you? You still haven't given me your top three gift wishes."

"I don't care, Mama," Toni said.

"What do you mean, you don't care? You've always cared!"

"I haven't thought about it much. I don't know."

Mrs. Douglas glanced at her wristwatch. "No time to go into this now. See you two later. Have a good day. I have to rush."

Toni bundled Carl up and hurried to meet Mattie at the corner.

"You ready for the big party?" asked Mattie, looking warily at her friend.

"Not really."

"Did you bring your present for the grab bag?"

"The grab bag?" Toni's eyes squinted.

"I called you yesterday to remind you."

"Oh, no, I forgot to get something!" Toni said. "I was going to, then I just forgot."

"You've been doing a lot of forgetting this week," said Mattie, taking Carl's hand as they crossed the street.

"I know," Toni said. "I don't know what's wrong with me, Mattie."

"I wore something special today." Mattie's voice faltered; even her breath crept gingerly along the frozen air. "See." And she opened the top of her coat.

Toni stared at the white T-shirt with the motto "I Love New York!"

"Why are you wearing that?"

"Because Susan gave it to me. I thought it would be nice to wear it," Mattie explained, hastily buttoning herself back up.

"You didn't even like Susan. Don't you feel like a hypocrite, Mattie?"

"Why are you getting mad at me? I thought you'd like it."

"You're wrong! Just because Susan's dead, you wear that shirt!" Toni yelled, stopping in the middle of the block. "You never even liked her! She was my friend, not yours!"

And, with that, Toni grabbed a wide-eyed Carl and marched off to school, leaving Mattie standing there.

Still angry two hours later, Toni angled away from Mattie, ignoring her bewildered expression. She huddled over her work.

"Toni, come up here, please," said Mrs. Swallow. Today she was dressed in a green felt skirt appliqued with Christmas trees, reindeer, including a Rudolph with a protruding red yarn nose, angels, Santa Claus, and gaily wrapped gifts with tiny satin ribbons trailing across red sequins.

All she needs are two strings of lights and she'll be a live Christmas tree, Toni thought.

"Toni, where's the rest of your homework?" Mrs. Swallow asked, picking up a hairpin from her desk.

"I handed in all of the problems."

"I only have two word problems, and our agreement was five a week."

"I did the other three, Mrs. Swallow. I thought they were here." Toni hunted through the crumpled sheets of paper.

"I believe you, but I need to see all of the work, so please redo them now."

"Now?"

"Yes, right now, Toni." Mrs. Swallow handed her a ditto sheet and some blank paper. "The room will be quiet, and you can concentrate."

Stomping back to her cluster, Toni wanted to explode!

It's not fair! I did the work! I don't want to stay here doing these problems while everybody else gets to go out for recess, she thought, knocking one of her books to the floor.

Instead of joining her for lunch, Mattie went and sat with Ida and her friends. Toni sulked. As had been her habit for the past week, she threw away most of her lunch, not even bothering to save a Christmas cupcake covered with sprinkles for Carl.

During the afternoon Christmas party, Toni hid in a corner next to the plants. The plate of cake, ice cream, and potato chips lay on her lap, untouched. She sipped a little of the red punch, tasting ginger ale. Mrs. Swallow was leading the class in Christmas songs. Mattie's voice made the words hang in the air like crystal ornaments on a tree. Finally Joseph turned on the record player to dance.

"Want to dance?" Raymond asked.

"Uh, no," Toni stammered. She watched as white cake, melting ice cream, and half of the potato chips slid off her plate, landing on her left shoe.

"I'll get that," Raymond said, scooping up the mess and tossing it into a nearby wastebasket. "You upset?" he asked.

Toni shrugged her shoulders.

"Is it the King test?"

Toni only half heard him.

"Right. I forgot part of the homework," she sputtered.

"Susan. The party today. Now I know," he said.

Out of nowhere, tears blurred her view of Raymond. She looked down at the traces of red frosting that smeared her gym shoes. Furtively she swiped at them, feeling even more like a jerk.

"Here, Toni." He handed her a handkerchief. "You know how Mom makes me carry one."

Gratefully Toni wiped her eyes and glasses, wishing for the millionth time that her parents would buy contact lenses for her or, at the very least, some glasses fit for a twelve-year-old. She'd had those since fourth grade!

"Thanks, Raymond." She folded the handkerchief into a neat square and held it toward him.

"Keep it. One less I have to carry."

"Yes, I really miss Susan." Toni's voice was a little

stronger. "Watching everybody dancing and celebrating Christmas seems wrong."

Now he was the silent one. After about five minutes, Raymond touched her hand and got up.

"See you later," he said. "Merry Christmas, Toni."

"Merry Christmas," Toni replied.

Before the bell rang, Mrs. Swallow gave each of the children a book. "I've chosen one especially for each of you," she said. "Have a lovely holiday. Remember to be grateful for this time of the year. I'll see you all in the New Year."

The class flew out of the room, except for Toni. She held a book about the Shanghai Museum Exhibition. Photographs of the Water Spurting Basin and Magic Mirror jumped out at her.

"I just want to remind you to try to study, Toni," Mrs. Swallow said, her hand resting on Toni's shoulder. "Most of your answers to the word problems were wrong, so we'll have a lot of work to do when you return. I know this is a difficult period for you. Try to have a happy Christmas."

"Thanks for the book, Mrs. Swallow," said Toni. "The pictures look just like what we saw."

"That was a happy day for this class, a delightful one, especially for you and Susan," her teacher said gently. "I wanted you to have a memento of our trip."

Toni thanked her again and left. Mattie wasn't outside the room, and Toni didn't see her waiting in the playground. She got Carl and started home.

A sense of recurring dread filled her as they stepped

off the curb to cross the street. Any minute a car careening around the corner or speeding through a red light could hit her and Carl, tossing them up into the air like puppets or, worse, dragging them down the icy street. She yanked Carl to safety, her heart thudding.

I hate being scared like this, she said to herself.

Once home, she felt safer. Each time she walked past the telephone, she thought about calling Mattie. Four years of being best friends was a long time. This was their worst fight ever. But she couldn't figure out what she wanted to say. "I'm sorry" wouldn't be enough.

The phone didn't ring. Except once.

"Hello. This is the Douglas residence," Toni answered, hoping to hear Mattie's voice.

"Hello. Toni, this is Father Lawrence. Are your parents home?" he replied, his voice distant.

"No, Father Lawrence, they're both working late."

"I see. Mother and I are back from Jackson. Everything went as well as can be expected." He paused. "But Mother is not doing well. I think being here for Christmas will be much too hard on us."

"Is Susan buried?" Toni asked.

"Yes, Toni. And it is a very lovely plot, under a large old tree not too far from a stream. Very lovely," he repeated. "I wanted your parents to know that I'm taking Mother to her sister's in California for Christmas."

"When will you be back?" Toni squeaked.

"Maybe in late January. I can't say for sure, Toni," he said. "Please tell your parents, and thank them for all their love and support."

"Yes, sure I will," Toni said, her stomach sinking. This would be the first time in two years they hadn't shared Christmas with the Lawrences. No turkey dinner with Mother Dear, none of Father Lawrence's famous eggnog—and no Susan.

"Thank you, Toni. How are you?" he asked.

"Okay." Tony squeezed back the tears. "I'll tell Daddy and Mama. Tell Mother Dear hello and Merry Christmas."

"That's right, Christmas is a few days away, isn't it?" His voice drooped. "The same to you, Toni. Good-bye."

Seeing tiny multicolored lights twinkling off and on, Toni checked the Christmas tree. Mama's fourteen-year collection of ornaments from all around the world dangled brightly from every branch. Already several wrapped gifts covered the velvet Christmas tree skirt.

Yesterday Mrs. Douglas and Toni had arranged the manger scene. Toni held up her favorite carved figure, Mary holding the baby Jesus. On the mantel, on either side of the figures, were two ivory candles in golden holders. On Christmas Eve, Carl would light one and Toni, the other. Gazing around the room, Toni smiled. Her father had hung the mistletoe early this year. He always did. "To make sure I get my share of kisses," he liked to say.

Where is that Carl? she wondered.

Toni found his curly head on his pillow. His arms were wrapped around his giraffe. He was exhausted from all of the excitement of the holiday. She slid his clothes off and his pj's on. Then she covered him up. She was glad that they'd eaten an early dinner.

With the house so still and no distractions, Toni looked around her room, noticing in the corner her unfinished present for Mattie. The wool cap in rich tones of rose and cream lay next to a partially completed matching scarf.

If I work hard, I can be through with Mattie's gift in time, Toni figured. She had hidden her gift for Susan under her bed last week.

Under the spell of the Christmas tree, Toni's hands deftly chained three and anchored each chain with a single crochet, creating a simple but striking pattern. One row of the shell stitches would edge the scarf. As she worked, her mind rested.

Every now and then, Toni stopped to stare at certain ornaments on the tree—the bamboo dove of peace from the Philippines, the little wooden girl in a swing, and the ceramic gingerbread boy. Beyond the misty front windows, thick, luxurious snowflakes sifted through the air like flour in a sieve.

When her parents came home, Toni was dozing on the couch. "Oh, Daddy, Mama, you're home." Toni roused herself, grabbing and pinning the crochet hook to the scarf so she wouldn't pull out any precious stitches. The scarf was much longer, revealing a couple of hours of intense effort.

"We're sorry, honey. We got stuck in the storm," said her mother, shaking the snow from her scarf and coat.

"Where's Carl? Any messages?" asked her father, bending down to kiss her.

Toni told them about the call from Father Lawrence, aware of the look that passed between her parents. Too tired to stay up and talk to them, she undressed and climbed into bed, but not before she peeked at the two pictures of Susan lying on top of the music box. Then she positioned the Teddy bear in the corner of her bed. The paper bag from Mother Dear lay carefully folded at the bottom of her drawer, next to the Statue of Liberty earrings and the breadsticks. Tucked under her pillow was Raymond's handkerchief.

When morning came, Toni yawned and scratched her head. The clock said noon!

"About time, sleepyhead." Her mother chuckled. "Carl's been up and out in the snow for hours."

Unable to stand the separation from Mattie any longer, Toni called her. "Hi, is Mattie home?" she asked Mattie's brother. The response was no. Mattie had gone out Christmas shopping!

And she didn't even call me! She could have called and invited me.

Four days later it was Christmas Eve. Toni had fought hard with herself. At last she decided to call her friend again.

"Mattie? Hi, it's me."

"Hi."

"Did you buy all your gifts?"

"Yeah."

"Me, too. Uh, Mattie?"

"Yeah."

"I'm sorry for what I said. I don't know, sometimes it seems as if I'm angry with you for no reason. Everything and everyone bugs me," Toni rushed on, making herself say it all. "It's as if something gets in my brain and makes scrambled eggs of it! I want us always to be friends, Mattie. But I miss Susan."

"Well, I miss my daddy, but I don't yell at you. You don't have the right to be mean to me, Toni," Mattie said. "I didn't hurt Susan."

"I never had anyone I loved die before, Mattie."

"Just because my father died doesn't qualify me as an expert," Mattie said. "I didn't want Susan to die, Toni, but I'm tired of you being nice to me one day and mean to me the next. This is a horrible time for me, too. Another Christmas without my father. Look, I have to study and clean house."

"I'm sorry, Mattie. I made a present for you," said Toni. There was a long stretch of silence.

"I have one for you, too," Mattie said.

"See you at church?"

"All right, Toni."

Toni didn't feel much better. Mattie's anger disturbed her. On Christmas Day Toni opened her gifts:

a gold chain necklace and earrings from her parents, as well as some cologne and clothes, and a drawing of Carl on a red bike from Carl. Her family enjoyed their gifts from her.

The sight of Carl trying to ride his bike up and down the hall tickled Toni. While he practiced, she ran down one flight of stairs. She knocked on the door, admiring the wreath of holly and pine cones.

"Merry Christmas, Toni my dear!" cried Mrs. Stamps, flinging open the door. Hannibal barked his greeting. Christmas music played on the radio. A small white tree with gold balls stood on the coffee table.

"Merry Christmas, Mrs. Stamps." They hugged.

"I'm so happy to see you on this blessed day. Please sit down. Here is your gift," said Mrs. Stamps.

"This is mine for you," replied Toni. "Carl is upstairs falling all over the place, trying to ride his bike."

"I know, I can hear him." She chuckled. "Oh, what a wonderful gift, and it has such a pure tone. Thank you, Toni my darling!" The elderly woman shook the small Christmas bell close to her ear, obviously pleased with the sound.

"Oh, Mrs. Stamps, this is so pretty." Holding up a bright red wool cardigan, Toni examined the buttons made of a clear plastic with red, blue, and green flowers painted inside. She tried on the sweater, relieved that it fit so well.

"Yes, I noticed that your shape is changing and allowed for that." Mrs. Stamps smiled. "You've had some chilly times lately, so this is something to keep you warm, inside and out. Now, tell me how you're doing."

Toni left Mrs. Stamps's apartment an hour later. Somehow, talking with her calmed Toni down. She was very glad that she had gone ahead and completed Mattie's present.

When she got home, she had to rush to get dressed for church. There Toni searched for Mattie. They sat together in the choir pews. Songs and prayers of celebration and blessings to the baby Jesus filled the church.

After the service, Toni handed Mattie an oblong package. Mattie gave her a square one.

"This is really pretty, Toni." Mattie tried on the hat and scarf, fingering the soft, lush wool yarn. "Thank you very much."

"Oh, no, you didn't have to do this," cried Toni, holding up the T-shirt Susan had given Mattie.

"I thought you would like to have something from Susan."

"But Susan gave the T-shirt to you," said Toni, pushing the shirt into Mattie's hands.

"She was just being nice," Mattie said, giving it back to Toni. "You were her real friend, Toni, not me. Merry Christmas."

Before school started in early January, Raymond called once. Toni talked with Mattie a couple of times over the holiday, but there wasn't much to share.

Toni spent her time reading and staring out of the window. Sometimes she thumbed through the Shanghai Museum Exhibition book, hearing Susan's laughter and seeing the reflected design from the Magic Mirror. Regularly she tried to work on the math problems.

Somehow she didn't expect to see Mattie on the corner by the mailbox that first Monday morning in January. But Mattie was there, wearing the hat and scarf. Carl hurled snowballs at the ground on the way to school. When Raymond called out to Toni, Mattie walked on.

"Hey, Toni, hi," called Raymond, running over to her.

"Hi, Raymond."

He dug into his pockets, then searched his notebook. Finally he handed her an envelope.

"I forgot to give you this."

Toni opened the envelope. There was a card and a Garfield eraser inside.

"Thanks," she murmured. "I don't have a present for you."

He shrugged. "The eraser is for good luck on the exams. See you later."

Carl ran up to her, waving good-bye to Raymond.

"Raymond's your boyfriend now," he said.

"Oh, Carl, don't be silly."

"What did he give you? He didn't give me a present."

"Just a card and an eraser."

"I have a girlfriend, Melanie. She's nice," Carl said. "I like having a girlfriend. She chases me, and I chase her."

"Good for you. Raymond is my friend, not my boyfriend. You understand, Carl?"

"No." He took off, sliding and slipping down the street.

Toni caught up with him. She grabbed Carl's hand and hollered at Mattie to wait for them.

The rest of the month lingered on like a toothache. Toni missed problems, often forgot her homework, and failed to answer questions during class discussions. Most of the time she felt too exhausted to think, and went to bed as soon as dinner was over.

One day toward the end of January, six weeks after the funeral, Mrs. Swallow told Toni to stay after school.

"But I have to get my little brother. He'll be scared if I'm not there," Toni protested.

"I know, and I've made arrangements for him to come up here and sit while I talk to you." Mrs. Swallow gestured to Toni to sit down in the chair by her desk. "Now, what's the matter?"

"Nothing."

"Something is. You're not trying anymore, Toni, not with math, not with anything," the teacher said. "You stare off into space, daydreaming all day long. You don't volunteer for anything. The entrance exam for King Academy is coming up in March and, with your present attitude, I don't think you're going to be able to pass."

Hearing the door open, Toni twisted around. Carl came in. Mrs. Swallow gave him some crayons and paper and sent him over to the media table at the back of the room.

"Toni, what are we going to do?" she asked, sitting down again.

"I don't know."

"What is it? What's going on inside that head of yours?"

Feeling like she was stuck in quicksand, Toni struggled to identify the source of her growing sense of despair. Nothing was familiar or safe. Nothing except her family and Mrs. Stamps and Hannibal.

"Toni, I can hear your mind whirling." Mrs. Swallow leaned closer. "Tell me what you're thinking."

"Everything is strange and different. I don't know what to do anymore." Toni fumbled for the right words.

Mrs. Swallow listened.

"Susan is dead. Just like that, she's here and then suddenly she's gone. Everybody goes on after the funeral is over like that's it—but it's not! I'm supposed to study to go to King. I'm supposed to pass that test! I can't just forget about Susan and go on like nothing happened!"

"Susan is dead, that's true. But you're mistaken if you believe that people just continue living as if her life had had no meaning," said Mrs. Swallow. "I miss her. I know that her parents will be sad for years, and her grandparents."

"What about the man who killed her? They should send him to jail forever, not three years at the most."

The teacher nodded.

"Mrs. Swallow, Susan would be fifteen in three years. Now she won't even be thirteen."

"No, she won't. And that is terrible."

Toni looked warily at Mrs. Swallow's earnest face.

"Toni, I'm afraid the way you're grieving for Susan is making life too hard for you. You need to remember that your life goes on. You have dreams to make come true."

"But what do I do? Act like everything is fine? Study hard?" she said, her hands twisting. "Be a good girl?"

"You have to come to terms with your loss," Mrs. Swallow said. "I care about you, and I'm here to listen whenever you want to talk. I do want you to get into King, Toni."

"Thanks, Mrs. Swallow. I have to go home." More confused than ever, Toni left with Carl.

"Hi." Mattie was standing outside.

"Hi, Mattie. Thanks for waiting," said Toni as Carl ran on.

"I didn't mind, Toni," Mattie said. "Did you get the speech that goes 'Now, Toni, I'm sorry your friend is dead, but you have to go on, make her proud of you, study hard, do well in school, etc., etc., etc.,' huh?"

Toni's mouth sprang open in amazement. "How did

you know? Did you hear Mrs. Swallow through the door?"

"No, I've been through that one," said Mattie. "When Daddy died, I had one grown-up after another lecturing me about how I had to make him proud of me, help my mother, go on."

"But you did."

"I was faking a lot of the time." She buttoned up her coat. "I cried for Daddy every single day and night. But only under my pillow, or in the bathroom with the water running so nobody heard."

"I didn't know that."

"I know."

Shame swept over Toni, making her blush in the cold. They had been best friends, and Mattie had been forced to hide her true feelings. Toni knew why. She hadn't wanted to know or to hear. It had been too terrifying to believe that she could lose her father or mother.

"So what did you do? How did you stop feeling lost and . . ." Toni groped for the words once more.

"And confused, and mad and tired and just blank?" said Mattie. "I'll tell you, because no matter what, we're still best friends."

Mattie took a deep breath, while Toni waited.

"Toni, the truth is that no matter how many people try to help you feel better, in the end you have to do the real work by yourself."

"What do you mean, 'the real work'?" Toni asked.

"Hmmm. Well, I had to figure out a way to go on even though Daddy was dead." Mattie faced Toni. "A way that I could still keep him and me, too."

"What did you do?"

"I made a special place for me and my daddy."

"A what?"

"Really two places. A place inside where I think about him, and also leave him when I have things to do. And a special place somewhere else." She stopped.

Toni was fascinated. Mattie had never talked like that before.

"Where?"

Mattie paused. "Look, I can't tell you about that. And, anyway, you'd never want to do what I did."

"Mattie, my heart hurts," Toni said.

"I know," Mattie said softly. Then her voice firmed. "I have some time today. You want to work on those word problems?"

"Yes, Mattie. And thanks for waiting for me."

Even as Toni walked along with Mattie, her mind was somewhere else, searching for a way to make a special place for Susan. Time was running out! The real entrance exam was just weeks away, and all she'd been doing was grieving over Susan.

I'm tired of being mixed up and miserable, Toni thought. *I want to feel like Mattie. But how? How?*

10

A Problem-Solving Exercise

Spotting Carl after school the following week was easy. In his colorful hat and snowsuit, Toni and Mattie couldn't miss him if they wanted to.

"Toni, Toni, George died today!" Carl shouted, running up to her.

"Yeah, he just fell over, plop, and he was dead," added Harry Edwards, his brown eyes huge. Jon Ella nodded in agreement.

Shocked, Toni frowned at Mattie. "Who's George?"

"You saw him every time you came to read to my class with Mattie," Carl said.

"I don't remember a kid named George. Do you?" Toni asked Mattie, who was pulling the rose and cream hat over her ears and tucking in the matching scarf.

The three first-graders whooped with laughter. And

Jon Ella began dancing around and singing, making
the boys join in:

> The worms crawl in,
> The worms crawl out,
> The worms play pinochle
> On your snout.
>
> They put you
> In a big, black box
> And cover you up
> With dirt and rocks.
>
> The worms crawl in
> The worms crawl out,
> The worms play pinochle
> On your snout.

Toni recognized the song. She and Mattie had
learned it one summer at camp. The rest of the verses
came back to her:

> And then you turn
> A gruesome green,
> And pus comes out
> Like shaving cream.
> The worms crawl in,
> The worms crawl out,
> The worms play pinochle
> On your snout.
> Never laugh when
> A hearse goes by

For you may be
The next to die!

"Yuck!" said Toni, glad for the first time that the pink and white casket had been closed tightly. "Carl, stop singing that horrible song and tell me who George is."

"Carl, I want to know, too," demanded Mattie, catching him by the arm.

"George is a gerbil! A boy gerbil!" crowed Carl. Then he became serious. "We had a funeral for him, right in the room."

"I was scared to touch him," Jon Ella said. "But I touched the box we put him in."

"We wrote George a good-bye letter, and then the teacher took him away," Carl said, his voice sad. Then his eyes lit up. "But she said we'll get a rabbit soon and I get to feed it!"

"I liked George." Harry Edwards sucked his thumb.

Toni shook her head, wondering what a cold thumb tasted like. A funeral in the room? What a strange idea.

After two hours of working with Mattie and dashing to the front window to call Carl to come in, Toni needed a break. Mattie agreed. They decided to have some cocoa.

"You're losing weight, Toni."

"I know. My whole body is changing. Getting bigger in some places and smaller in others."

"I wish mine was. I'm doomed to be a blah, skinny

girl," Mattie said, sighing. "My mother laughed at me when I asked her if I could get a bra. Do you know what she said?"

"No." Toni lowered herself into the chair next to Mattie, not wanting to miss a single word.

"She said I didn't have anything to put in a bra. She told me to wait two or three years. By then every girl in the world will be wearing a bra except me!"

"You want to wear one of mine?" offered Toni.

"Really? Could I? I never even tried one on."

Happier, Mattie left with the pink bra wrapped in tissue paper and stuffed into her purse. Afterward Toni fingered the white bra that Susan had given her. Instead of finishing her homework, she lay down and closed her eyes.

During dinner that evening, the phone rang and her father answered it. He returned to the table with a serious face.

"That was Mrs. Swallow."

Toni pushed a green bean to the other side of her plate.

"She's very upset. She told me that unless you buckle down and work, you won't pass the test and get into King," he said, looming over her. "Your teacher is very concerned about the way you're acting. Frankly, so are we."

Toni fixed her attention on the kitchen window and the dark winter night. *Why can't they just leave me alone? Stop picking on me about that dumb test and King.* She hid her face so they couldn't read her thoughts.

"Toni, two months have gone by. You are *worse,*" her mother said. "And we don't know what to do. We leave you alone, and you sleep all the time. We try to talk to you, and you stare out the window."

The silence that followed enveloped the family. Faint sounds of the TV and Carl's laughter drifted in and out.

"Can I please be excused?" Toni asked.

"Harold, can you think of anything to say?"

Mr. Douglas shook his head.

"Can I go to my room?" Toni asked.

"All right, Toni, go on. But we're not through with this," her father said.

Mrs. Swallow was absent the next morning. When she returned in the afternoon, she called the bottom math group together.

"This morning I attended the last in a series of five special math workshops. I have something wonderful to teach you!" she said, laying out blank sheets of paper and crayons.

Toni rolled her eyes to the ceiling. *Another one of Mrs. Swallow's baby games! Well, I'm not going to play this time.*

Despite her lack of enthusiasm, Toni went along with the lesson. Mrs. Swallow had learned a new way to teach them how to understand math word problems. Toni reread the steps on the ditto sheet before her. Read the problem three times and underline the math words. Circle the numbers and draw a box around what the problem asks you to do. Then state the problem in your own words. Ask yourself, what do they want to know?

Toni laughed at the next step. Draw a picture of the problem. Then set up the problem and estimate the answer. Check the answers on the test to see if one is close to your estimate. Finally solve the problem and ask yourself, "Does this answer make sense?" If your answer makes sense, compare it to your estimate. Pick the response on the test that is closest.

Toni shook her head. *Wow! By the time I'm through doing all this, the test will be over!*

"Okay, what's the answer to number one? Write your answer on your personal chalkboard right under your estimate."

The six children in the group did that. Unconvinced, Toni followed their lead. She looked around the group. Her answer agreed with that of two others.

"Toni, Joseph, and Latwanda, you are correct! Now, the rest of you, that was a good try. This is a hard problem. Let's see where you got off the track."

Startled, Toni reexamined her answer. She was right! And she understood the problem. She listened as the teacher went over the responses of the kids who had failed to get the correct answer. Best of all, she understood where they had gotten confused.

When Mrs. Swallow called on her to explain the second problem, Toni was right again! But the whole process took so long! Toni bit her lip. The King entrance examination was timed. She wouldn't have fifteen minutes to talk to herself and draw pictures!

"Group, we have to stop now. Here are the five problems I want you to do for homework," Mrs. Swallow said. "And I want you to do every step. Pictures, too."

"But it takes so long," Toni complained. "We won't have time to do all this on the test."

"Yes, you will. If you work hard and practice the steps."

"Is seven weeks enough time to get fast?" Toni asked.

"That depends on you." Mrs. Swallow passed out the homework and dismissed the group.

While the gym class played volleyball, Toni kept hearing the words from Jon Ella's worm song. Scenes from the funeral flashed through her mind.

Why isn't the funeral enough for me? she thought. *What's missing?*

The boos from her teammates yanked her back to reality. She had missed an easy hit. Then something hit *her*. She knew whom she had to see.

Since Mattie had to face another trip to the dentist after school, Toni and Carl walked home without her. Toni ran upstairs and checked her mother's note. She slapped a bologna sandwich together for Carl and hurried through her chores. Then she grabbed Carl and headed downstairs.

Toni rang the buzzer three times, giving up just as the door opened. Mrs. Stamps was breathing hard.

"Come in, Toni my dear and Carl darling," she huffed. "I just completed twenty minutes riding through the south of France, and I was making a cup of lemon tea."

Carl kissed her perspiring cheek and ran for Hannibal and his toy box. Toni followed Mrs. Stamps back to the kitchen.

"That sweater looks lovely on you," said Mrs. Stamps, taking out two flowered china cups with handles shaped like butterflies.

"Thank you. Uh, I wanted to talk to you," began Toni, perching on a stool under the clock.

"Fine, go ahead. My dinner is fixed and my gentleman friend is not due for supper until seven." Mrs. Stamps poured the tea and set out a plate of wheat crackers and cheddar cheese.

A gentleman friend? Does Mrs. Stamps have a boyfriend? Toni was shocked. *Well, it figures. Mrs. Stamps is different from any grown-up I know.*

"Mrs. Stamps, will I ever be happy again, like I used to be?" she blurted out.

The old lady stopped. Her arms surrounded Toni.

"My, what a powerful question for someone so young," she murmured. "Yes, Toni my dear. Maybe not soon, but one day you will be happy."

"How do you know?" Toni dared to probe, knowing that Mrs. Stamps wouldn't talk down to her.

"Because what has happened to you has happened to me, many times," she said, moving to sit down.

"Your best friend died?"

"Oh, yes. And two husbands, my father, mother, and sister. They are all gone," said Mrs. Stamps.

"That's horrible. All of them?" Toni was stunned. *How can she stand losing her whole family?*

"In this life you have two choices, Toni," said the elderly woman. "You get old or you die young. If you live long enough, you see many of the people you love die. That's life."

Toni thought. "How did you get happy again?" she asked.

Mrs. Stamps rested her chin on her hand, silent and still for a long time. Toni waited. That was another thing she liked about Mrs. Stamps. She let her words out carefully instead of throwing them like rocks or missiles.

"I took the time to mourn in my own way," she said. "And I decided to let that person go and keep the memories in my heart. I made myself return to the business of living."

Toni didn't understand what she meant, and her confusion showed on her face. "Can Mother Dear and Father Lawrence do that?" she asked.

"I don't know. Their grief and Susan's parents' is beyond forgetting, but maybe not beyond healing," she reflected, sipping the tea.

"How?"

"With time, work, love, and faith. But you are really asking me about you, aren't you?"

"Yes," Toni answered.

"You have to make your own peace, and that takes doing, not sitting around and moping. *Doing.*" Mrs. Stamps's eyes twinkled.

Back in the apartment, Toni took out the Statue of Liberty earrings, the photos, the T-shirt, and other mementos. *What am I supposed to do?* For once talking to Mrs. Stamps hadn't given her the answers.

I need to talk to Mattie. Toni slumped down. *Do I dare call her and ask her about something she told me she wouldn't talk about?* The truth was that there was nobody else to turn to.

Hoping that Mattie would listen, Toni called. "Mattie, it's me."

"Did I forget something?" asked Mattie.

"No, I need you to help me, Mattie. Look, before you say no, I know that I've been acting strange for a while," Toni said. "And I'm sorry, but I still don't know what to do about Susan and the way I feel. I'm stuck."

"You mean you want me to tell you what I did after my father died?"

Toni took a deep breath. "Yes, please, Mattie."

"Well, maybe knowing what I did can help you," Mattie said.

Toni's heart skipped. She yelled to Carl to turn down the TV.

"You sure you won't think I was silly?" Mattie asked.

"Cross my heart, I promise, I swear."

Mattie took a deep breath. "Now, you have to promise not to tell anybody, and I mean not a living soul!"

"I swear I won't, Mattie."

"Okay. After the funeral, I kept up my schoolwork and all, but inside I was a mess. So I had my own special funeral for my daddy. Just me," Mattie stressed. "I planned the service." Then she stopped.

"Please, Mattie, tell me what you did."

"Remember, this is our most important secret," she said, not continuing until Toni had reassured her. "Well, there was the wake and funeral, just like for Susan. I went, but the services were more for Mom and Grandmama than me. I don't know. I felt so bad seeing my daddy in the coffin and then them putting him in the ground. Then coming home every day and not seeing him. Waking up in the morning and him not being there. For a while I believed that his getting killed was my fault. I made him die. I did something wrong. But I don't believe that now."

"Me, too. Sometimes I dream that Susan is crossing the street and I'm shouting to her to stop, but she keeps going," Toni said. "And I get scared when I think about her and I can't remember her face."

"Yeah, I know about that. That's why I keep a picture of my daddy in my room. I get so scared when I think I might forget what he looked like."

Toni kept quiet, hoping she would go on.

"The rest is that I made my own funeral for him. His real grave is far away and I can't get there on the bus. I took some things and made him special presents. I went to a place in the park that we used to go to, under a ginkgo tree. And I buried the presents with a note to him and then I . . . "

"Don't stop now!"

"I sang some songs, his favorites and mine. And whenever I really need to, I go there and sit awhile," she said. "When I leave, I feel better."

"And nobody knows about this but me?"

"Just you and my brother. Mom would get upset, so I don't tell her."

"I won't tell anyone. I promise, Mattie. That's really something, what you did," Toni said, feeling a new respect for Mattie.

"So if you don't like being stuck, why don't you unstick yourself?"

"I don't know what to do."

"Well, you have to figure that out. Think about it, like I did," Mattie said. "I have to finish my homework. See you later."

Toni's head was spinning. *I can't wait until spring. There aren't any special trees around here. The ground is frozen. I can't dig a hole.*

Stymied, Toni tackled the word problems, using the new method. Discouraged because the process took so long, she slammed the book shut. Deep into the night she thought, disturbed only by the hum of her parents' voices.

They sound so serious, Toni thought, hearing the sound of her name a few times.

Unable to go to sleep, Toni sat up in bed. *Find a special place? I don't have one, except for the lake. That was Susan's favorite, too.*

In the moonlight, Toni stared at a photo of herself and Susan at the beach. *I don't have much time, with the test coming up.*

As she slid down and drew the covers around her shoulders, the beginnings of a plan blossomed in her head.

11

Unexpected Factors

After breakfast on a cloudy Wednesday morning, Toni prepared for school. She checked the calendar for her next period, just as her mother had suggested. She couldn't help seeing the big red X on March 26, which marked the date for the exam.

If we moved into King's district, I could get in without having to take the test. Toni knew she was grasping at straws. *Or if Daddy used somebody's address in the district, then I could get in by pretending I lived near the school.* Her parents would never agree to that idea.

But what if I get scared and freeze up? What if I forget how to do the steps? What if I fail? She looked dejectedly at the mementos from Mother Dear. Spending her time thinking about Susan hadn't been helping her prepare for the test. She had to move fast.

A quick glance out the window told her that today would be a good day to put her plan into action. The air was still. The trees weren't whipping in the wind. The sky lay like a light blue shell over the buildings. Today.

"Toni, you're not going to school this morning," announced Mrs. Douglas, standing in the doorway, dressed for work.

"Why not, Mama? I feel fine."

"Because your father and I have planned a trip for you," she said.

Bewildered, Toni followed her mother into the living room, where her father sat, going through some papers in his briefcase. His face was drawn from late nights of studying. When his eyes focused on her, the fatigue in them shocked Toni. She realized that she hadn't paid much attention to him in the past several weeks.

"Honey, we've arranged for you to spend the morning at King Academy," he said, making room for her near him.

"King Academy?"

"I wanted to take you myself, but I'm swamped at work." He rubbed his eyes. "So your mother is going to drive you there and then take you to school. Don't worry, we called Walker this morning."

"But I'm not supposed to go to King until I pass the test," Toni said. "And I have to go to school today."

"You can go this afternoon, Pumpkin," replied her

father. "Your mother and I hope that a tour of King will lift your spirits."

Seeing the expectant smiles on their faces and feeling a sense of anticipation, Toni jumped up. She would have to postpone acting on her plan until tomorrow.

"This is a surprise. I've never been inside King. But I can't wear these clothes. I have to change."

"We have to leave soon, so hurry up," her mother called.

Toni yanked one outfit after another from her closet. *Something simple is best. Then I can blend in,* she thought. *I don't want to look like I don't belong.* Finally she made a choice and dressed. Her mother was knocking on her door!

The grounds of King Academy were crowded with kids laughing, talking, listening to radios. All kinds of kids: black, white, Asian. Toni's eyes were the size of half dollars as she stared at the clothes, hairstyles, and makeup.

The building took up most of the block. Over the main entrance, engraved letters spelled out "Dr. Martin Luther King, Jr., Academy." Hundreds of students filed into the large corridor to their lockers.

Toni and her mother walked to the main office. Gray metal lockers in two tiers lined both sides of the hallway. Unobtrusively Toni turned to see what was in them. She saw one black girl quickly key in her combination, whip off the lock, grab a stack of books, and stuff her coat into the space. *Imagine having my own secret combination and locker!* thought Toni.

The main office was bustling and far larger than the one at Walker Elementary. Bells rang loudly. More kids streamed in and out of the room. Adults and students moved like pedestrians in rush-hour traffic.

"Hello, Dot, so good to see you," said an official-looking black man, stout, with a full beard. "It's been a long time."

"Too long, Dr. Lewis," said Toni's mother. "This is my daughter, Antoinette. We call her Toni."

"Hello, Antoinette," he said, shaking Toni's hand. "Let's go into my office."

Toni was ushered into another large room with a huge rectangular desk. Wooden chairs, plants, and colorful posters created a warm ambience. Toni especially liked the poster depicting a powerful sailboat in the middle of an ocean. The sail billowed out in stripes of turquoise, red, and green. The caption read "Sail the seas of life."

"Now, no more Dr. Lewis, Dot," he said. "You knew me when I was a poverty-stricken graduate student. If it hadn't been for your generosity, I would never have gotten my dissertation typed in time to graduate."

Confused, Toni stared at her mother.

"Oh, Marvin, don't make so much of it." Mrs. Douglas laughed.

"Antoinette, do you know that your mother typed a two-hundred-page dissertation for about fifty dollars?" he said. "I didn't have enough money to pay her all at once. In fact, it took me over a year to pay you, Dot, and you didn't make it easier by refusing to take the money."

They chuckled together.

"How's Harold?" he asked.

"Fine. Exhausted, though, from studying for his CPA exam in May," she admitted.

"I know he'll pass. Now, Antoinette, I understand that if you score high on the city exam, you'll be a student at King in the fall?"

Toni nodded.

"Excellent. I've arranged for one of our students to take you on a tour of our school this morning. You'll attend classes with her and have lunch. Then your mother will pick you up here," he told her. "I hope you have a good morning. King Academy is an outstanding school. I'm sure you'd fit in here just fine." His confident smile included Toni and her mother.

"But, Mama, I thought you were going with me."

"No, honey, not this time." Mrs. Douglas reached out for Toni's hand.

She started at the rap on the door. When Dr. Lewis said "Enter," the door opened. Toni saw a white girl with a head full of red curls. The girl was wearing dark wool slacks and a plaid blouse with a blazer. Toni was glad that she had changed into her wool slacks, a blue ivy-league shirt, and the red sweater from Mrs. Stamps.

"Good morning, Erin," said Dr. Lewis. "This is Mrs. Douglas and her daughter, Antoinette. Or do you prefer 'Toni'?"

Startling herself, Toni answered, "No, sir, Antoinette is fine." She caught her mother's smile. Antoinette sounded more sophisticated.

"Hello, Mrs. Douglas and Antoinette," Erin said, shaking their hands. "Nice to meet you."

"Now, Erin, bring Antoinette back to the main office right after lunch."

"No problem, Dr. Lewis." Erin grinned at Toni. "Antoinette, I have room in my locker for your jacket. We have to run to my first-period class."

Hoping that her mother wouldn't kiss her, Toni jumped up and walked to the door. But she couldn't leave without waving good-bye. Mrs. Douglas waved back.

Erin called hi to lots of kids as they dashed to her locker. It seemed as if she knew everybody.

"I'm in the ninth grade, and I was one of the 'early birds,' too," said Erin, closing her locker and heading for the stairs. "Just like you."

"What's an 'early bird'?" Toni asked.

"A kid who starts here in the seventh grade. My first class is double honors English," she said. "Mrs. Simmons is a nut about the Junior Great Books Program." Seeing Toni's puzzled expression, she grinned. "That's exactly the way I reacted. Antoinette, that's a pretty name. French, isn't it? Oh, back to the subject,

Junior Great Books. It just means that we read a lot and talk about what we read. And write essays! Tons of essays!"

"What are you reading today?" Toni hoped she was asking the right question.

"Tolstoy's *The Death of Ivan Illych*—a hard one." Erin opened the door. "A substitution for one of the regular readings. You sit by me."

The classroom was smaller than Toni's. She searched for desks, not seeing any. Instead an unruly semi-circle of chairs with arms to write on faced the front of the room. On the blackboard was one question written in bold script. Aware of the curious glances of the teenagers, Toni slid into the chair next to Erin's and concentrated on the question: "Why doesn't the health and strength of the peasant Gerasim mortify Ivan Illych?"

Just then a young black woman dressed in a lemon-colored knit suit came in. She was carrying a leather briefcase.

"Just relax. Nobody's going to hassle you, Antoinette," said Erin. "You're my guest."

Toni looked into Erin's green eyes cautiously. Walker Elementary was all black. Toni was not used to being around white kids. It helped to see other black students in the class, at ease with their white and Asian peers.

As Mrs. Simmons took her chair, the class hushed. Erin raised her hand. "Mrs. Simmons, class, I'd like to introduce my guest, Antoinette Douglas. She'll be starting King next fall," said Erin, smiling.

If the floor had opened up and swallowed Toni, she would have fallen to her knees and given thanks. Her stomach plummeted! All those eyes on her! Barely hearing the welcome from Mrs. Simmons and the others, she bobbed her head, trying to smile at the same time.

However, an hour later, Toni was fascinated. She struggled to follow the flow of the discussion. Mrs. Simmons asked hard questions and forced her students to support their points by reading sections from the story. Toni was relieved when Erin got a nod of approval from the teacher after a particularly spirited exchange.

From that class, they went to biology lab. On the way Toni saw more boys than she'd ever seen. All kinds of boys: tall, short, cute, not so cute. Boys were everywhere! Toni wondered if Erin had a boyfriend, but she didn't dare ask. In the biology lab, Toni helped Erin dissect a frog. Not wanting to look scared, Toni held back the ligaments gingerly with a small knifelike tool, while Erin probed the leg.

"I'm trying to decide whether I want to be a pediatrician or an environmental biologist," Erin said, writing notes in her lab workbook. "What do you want to be, Antoinette?"

"A foreign journalist."

Erin glanced at Toni with admiration. "That's some

career! How did you decide on that?"

Toni hesitated and then settled on a "Susan-type" reply.

"I love to travel, and I'm good at writing." There was a lot of truth there. She just had never put it that way before.

"That's great, knowing what you're good at. I didn't know until this year." They smiled at each other.

"Trig is next. Then we go to the auditorium. I'm in the drama club, and we're putting on a play next month. Then lunch," said Erin. Erin stopped to talk to a black girl who looked like an older version of Mattie. "Cheryl, this is Antoinette. I'm her hostess today. Antoinette, this is my friend Cheryl."

While they talked, Toni wondered what trig was. She found out when they entered a larger classroom on the third floor. This time the blackboard was filled with incomprehensible symbols. They meant only one thing—math!

"I used to dread math," Erin said. "Then I got a teacher who really turned me on to thinking mathematically."

"What do you do about getting good scores on tests?" whispered Toni.

Erin laughed. "I study hard, do all the homework, and meditate."

"Meditate? What's that?"

"I'll tell you later. Mrs. Goldstein doesn't allow any talking in her class."

In the auditorium Erin waited to be called up to rehearse her part in a musical comedy written by the students. Compared to the auditorium at Walker Elementary, which doubled as the school lunchroom, this one was spectacular. Toni visualized Mattie singing the lead in the musical. She would be wonderful.

"You wanted to know what I meant when I told you that I meditate before and sometimes during trig tests," said Erin. "Cheryl should be the one to explain this, because she taught me how to meditate, but she's not here. We'll see her at lunch."

Toni listened.

"The night before the test, I close my eyes and sit real still in a quiet place." Erin stared at Toni, her green eyes serious. "Some people say you need to light a candle, but I don't use one. I close my eyes and repeat over and over again 'I will use the test to show what I know.' Or something positive and reaffirming like that. You follow me? My kind of mantra."

"You say this mantra over and over again? To yourself or whispering?"

"I like to say my mantra to myself, but do whatever suits you. Yes, I repeat it over and over," answered Erin. "Now, while I'm doing that, I make a picture in my mind. Pretend your mind is a blank TV screen is the way Cheryl puts it. On that blank screen, I make an image of myself taking the test and getting every problem right."

"How long does all this take?" Toni had images of

herself meditating all night and getting up in the morning too exhausted to write her name.

"Maybe ten minutes. Then I do the whole thing again the morning of the test, and if I lose control during the test"—Erin paused to see if she had to take her place on stage—"I take deep, slow breaths and keep the faith, like Cheryl says. I've got to get up there!"

Meditate. Toni rolled the word around in her head. She practiced making a TV screen while Erin was on stage. When Toni tired of mantras and TV screens, she watched the student actors. They were very serious.

When Erin returned for her, Toni hoped that the next destination was the lunchroom.

"I'm starving," Erin said.

"Me, too!" Toni laughed.

After a brief stop at the locker to drop off some books, they walked down a long hall to the lunchroom. Toni asked Erin where the computer room was. Erin detoured to the left and led Toni to a large room full of computer terminals and printers. Toni grinned. *Raymond will love this,* she thought, as she and Erin went to eat.

"Hot dogs or hamburgers, sandwiches or a hot lunch?" asked Erin, grabbing a tray for Toni as they stood amid a throng of kids.

"You mean you get choices here?"

"You sure do, and a couple of them are good." Erin smiled.

The excitement of the morning continued unabated at the lunch table. The table was crowded with Erin's friends: a Japanese boy named Michael, Cheryl, a couple of white girls, Tiffany and Anne, and John, who was black and a vegetarian. Toni thought John was cute. She had trouble remembering all of the names and following the rapid jokes, bits of gossip, quips, and plans that ran like rivulets from one side of the table to the other. But it felt wonderful to be there.

By the time Erin guided her back to the office and said good-bye, another of the many bells rang. There, in a seat by the door, waited her mother.

"Mama!" Toni ran to her, not caring if anybody saw them hug or not.

"How was your morning? I've been thinking about you all morning, going crazy with curiosity, Toni—or should I say Antoinette?"

Toni grinned. Her mother never missed a beat!

"It was fun, Mama, great. King is so big. And there's so much to learn." Toni didn't stop talking until they pulled up to her elementary school.

"I've been doing some thinking this morning, too." Mrs. Douglas twisted in her seat to face her daughter. "Your father and I have told you everything during this time except for one thing, that we love you."

"I know you do, Mama."

"Knowing isn't enough. You need to hear it more from us," she said. "We love you so much, Toni."

"I love you and Daddy, Mama."

"I need to hear that, too. But what I want to tell

you is that you have to want to go to King, Toni."
Her mother said each word slowly. "The truth is that
Susan was your first experience with death, but she
won't be your last."

"You mean you could die, or Daddy, or Carl, or
Mattie?" The names hurt coming out.

"Yes, that's what I mean, honey. But don't worry,
we all plan to live a long, long time."

Strangely enough, the quiet, empty halls at Walker
Elementary School soothed Toni. She had experienced
too much in one morning: new words like trig and
meditation; new choices, running the gamut from the
food she could eat for lunch to the career she could
prepare for; all kinds of kids—whites, Asians, His-
panics; and all those subjects and demanding teachers.

Gratefully Toni dropped into her seat, finding the
clusters of desks, the list of monitors on the blackboard, Mrs. Swallow's messy hair, even her math
group gathered in the front of the room reassuring. It
was like coming home from a hard day.

Raymond's name was on the sick list. Joseph told
her that he was out with the flu. Toni made a mental
note to call him after school. Once she told him about
King's computers, Raymond would feel great.

"Where have you been, Toni?" Mattie asked.

"At King Academy," Toni said. "Mama took me to
King today, and I went on a tour of the whole school
with a white girl named Erin."

Toni giggled at her expression. Mattie's mouth had
hit the floor!

"You what? How? What was it like?"

"I'll tell you later."

At the end of the school day, Toni promised Mattie that she'd call and tell her every detail. Then she and Carl took off, walking past Susan's house. Toni stood there. Even though it was mid-February, Father Lawrence and Mother Dear were still in California. Heavy drapes drawn across each window reminded her of the funeral home, but this time she knew there was nothing scary to hide.

And if I ring the bell, no one will answer, she thought, taking Carl's hand and turning for home.

Before Toni started her work, she called Raymond. With a sore throat and a fever over one hundred degrees, he could hardly talk. She offered to get the homework assignments for him. She thought about inviting him to join her tomorrow, even though she realized he wouldn't be able to. Still, she knew it would be wrong. Tomorrow was just for her, Carl, Mrs. Stamps, and maybe Mattie.

Tomorrow will be a very special day, Toni thought. She collected all of the things she would need to carry out her plan, and then made a quick visit to Mrs. Stamps. When Toni returned, she closed the door to her room and took out a sheet of Susan's stationery. Taking a deep breath, she sat down at her desk and began to write a letter. Several times Toni stopped to wipe her eyes. After placing the letter with the pile of items by the foot of her bed, she opened the door. Then she placed the promised call to Mattie.

That night, following Erin's directions, Toni sat in bed and began whispering, "I will use the test to show what I know," while she created a picture of herself solving each problem.

But the final image on her internal screen was of Susan and what she had to do. Tomorrow.

12

Symbols and Signs

*T*wo candles . . . matches . . . candleholders . . . the pictures . . . Statue of Liberty earrings . . . the T-shirt . . . bow ribbon . . . pens and pencils . . . the yellow stationery . . . and a paper bag.

Toni checked off the items, placing them in a bag while Carl finished his breakfast. Two things were missing. The music box was on top of her desk, and the breadsticks were in her bottom drawer. She went to the kitchen closet and took out the soup pot. Luckily her mother and father had left for work early.

During the walk to school, Toni went over her plan. She had a big decision to make. Toni pursed her lips. Should she invite Mattie? Would Mattie come if she asked her?

There she was on the corner, waiting for Toni just

as she'd promised to. That and their years of friendship settled the matter. Toni thrust the "I Love New York!" T-shirt into Mattie's hand.

"Susan gave this to you," Toni said, her voice firm.

Mattie smiled. "Thanks. I feel guilty about the whole thing, mostly how I felt about Susan. Maybe part of it was jealousy, Toni. She had everything and didn't appreciate it."

"You're wrong, Mattie, she didn't have everything," said Toni, remembering the phone call from Susan's mother and the "fantastic" trip to New York. "Anyway, I made up my mind to do something like what you did for your father."

"By yourself?"

"No, I need you, Carl, and Mrs. Stamps."

"When?"

"Today, at lunchtime. I'll have to be late to school this afternoon. Will you take Carl back to school for me?" she asked, breathing deeply.

"Sure." Mattie's smile was sad.

"Carl, you want to come to Mrs. Stamps's with me and Mattie at lunchtime?"

"Why?" he asked.

"To say good-bye to Susan." Toni bent down closer to him.

"I miss Susie," he said. "Yes, I want to come with you, Toni."

"This has to be our secret, Carl. Daddy and Mama can't find out."

"Then we have to do thumbs," he said, taking off his mittens. "Mattie, too!"

Shaking their heads, the girls put out their thumbs.

Part of the morning math time was devoted to taking mock tests. Toni chewed her eraser to a nub and forgot to meditate. She knew something that no one in the room was aware of. Today was Susan's birthday. *Mattie was right about birthdays,* she thought. *They hurt.*

When Toni and Mattie came around the corner at lunchtime, Carl was waiting by the swings. During the visit to Mrs. Stamps yesterday afternoon, Toni had worked out the order of the service. And she had dropped off everything there before she went to school.

The trio was silent when they reached their destination. Mrs. Stamps opened the door, smiling sweetly. Toni felt awkward. Maybe this wasn't a good idea.

"Hello, Toni, Mattie, Carl," she said. "Come in."

Toni led the group in.

"Now, Toni my dear, I know that this is your service. . . . " She took their coats, scarves, and hats. "But I must confess there is one little thing that I did and I hope you won't mind."

"What is it?" Toni asked.

"I made some lunch for afterward and a little gift."

"Thank you so much! I forgot about food!" Toni said. "Can we go in the dining room now? And eat later?"

While the group stood quietly, Toni took out the contents of the bag. She put the candles in their holders and lit them. Then she placed the pictures of Susan between them, propping them up with a couple of glasses. One by one she laid out the rest of the items: the stationery, the earrings, the bow ribbon from the Teddy bear, and a package of breadsticks.

"Okay." She took another deep breath. "I'd like each of us to write something nice about Susan, nice and true on the stationery. That's first."

Obediently the group settled around the table with the pens and pencils Toni supplied. Carl couldn't write well, so he drew a picture. Mrs. Stamps patted Hannibal off and on as she wrote her offering, while Toni held in her hand the letter she had written last night. Mattie got up once to look at the pictures.

"Now I want you to read yours aloud. And then we'll burn them in this pot."

"I want to go first," said Carl, standing up before the little shrine. "This is a picture of me and Susie playing on the swings, and I drew lemon drops all over."

He handed Toni the drawing and a lemon drop.

"I'll go next," volunteered Mrs. Stamps. " 'Dearest Susan, the Bible says that there is a season for everything, but your season ended too soon. I miss your beautiful face and vitality. God bless you and happy birthday. Love, Elvira Stamps.' "

"How did you know it was Susan's birthday?" Toni asked.

"Mother Dear called me from California last night,

very upset and depressed," Mrs. Stamps explained, folding her note and passing it to Toni.

"I guess I'm next," Mattie said. " 'Dear Susan, you know that we didn't get along real well, I guess because we were so different. But I miss seeing you. Being at school is not as exciting as when you were there. I miss the way you made me laugh, even when I didn't want to. Mattie.' "

Toni added Mattie's note to the small pile and then read her own. " 'Dear Susan, you were my best friend with Mattie for over two years. I miss you so much. I hate the man who killed you. I will keep our secrets forever. I will never forget you. I will always love you. Toni.' "

Trembling and crying, Toni folded the last note. Then she placed them all in her mother's iron soup pot.

"Now the last part. Mattie, will you sing something pretty?"

Mattie stood uneasily. Mrs. Stamps whispered something in her ear and Mattie straightened up. Softly the words to "Jesus Wants Me for a Sunbeam" filled the room. Toni lit a match and, under the watchful eye of Mrs. Stamps, burned the notes. The ashes fluttered in the pot.

"Thanks, Mattie. That was just right. Now we can eat, and then I have to go to the lake," said Toni. "I'll catch the bus to school."

"I'd feel so much better if I drove you," said Mrs.

Stamps. "I can wait in the car while you do what you must."

Seeing their anxious faces, Toni agreed. While the ashes cooled, Mrs. Stamps served lunch. Then Toni brushed the ashes into a small paper bag. It was the same one in which Mother Dear had placed the mementos of Susan. Mrs. Stamps came in with a small cake. "I thought we could also celebrate the fact that Susan was born and the time we had with her," she said, looking at Toni for approval.

"A birthday cake! Oh, Mrs. Stamps, I like that," Toni said.

While Mrs. Stamps locked up the apartment, Toni packed everything. Mattie's good-bye kiss on her cheek, light and brief, and Carl's hug were like anchors, keeping Toni steady and ready to take the next step.

Looking like a king, Hannibal sat in the back seat as Toni directed Mrs. Stamps to the pedestrian bridge by the lake. The wind was high, buffeting the car.

Despite her warm clothes, Toni was bitterly cold. She tried to stop her teeth from chattering. Toni gazed out at the gray mass of churning waves. Ignoring the Keep Out sign, she fought the wind to get closer to the water's edge. A mass of boulders jutted out into the lake, snatching the spray from the high waves. Seeing a way up, Toni climbed the slippery rocks.

The wind abated as she faced south, toward Jackson, Mississippi. Inch by inch she opened the bag and scooped out the ashes. With a silent prayer for Susan, Toni's arm reached out over the edge of the rocks, and slowly she opened her cold hand. The ashes danced over the waves.

Then Toni took out a special box, the music box from her grandmother. She touched the hand-painted lilies. Inside, on the velvet lining, rested the bow ribbon, one Statue of Liberty earring, and one breadstick snapped in half. Toni wound up the box.

When the tinkling music was loudest and clearest, she cast the box out, watching it bob on the waves until she could no longer see it. Finally, numb with cold, Toni clambered down the rocks, pausing to take one more look before running for the warmth of the car.

"Here's some tissues for your nose and your eyes, Toni," said Mrs. Stamps. "And I wrote a note to your teacher, saying that you ran an errand for me."

"Thank you," Toni said. "I didn't think about that."

"So? How do you feel now?"

Toni hesitated before answering. "I still feel sad. But I don't feel so stuck. I did something for Susan my way," Toni said. "Nobody can make me forget her. She was my best friend."

Mrs. Stamps nodded. "Learning to live with sorrow takes time and work. I'm sure you're on your way, Toni my dear."

Toni stared out the window. They were taking the

same route that the driver had taken to the funeral. The funeral seemed so long ago.

"I'm very proud of you." Mrs. Stamps spoke deliberately. "Very proud of you. I think your service was lovely, and I will always treasure being included. Thank you."

Hannibal growled and thrust his head and paws on Toni's head, licking her hair. She smiled a little.

When the exam was one week away, Toni asked Mattie about going to King Academy. "Mattie, are you worried about making it at King?"

"Nope," replied Mattie as the bell rang.

"Why not? You should see that place, Mattie. King is nothing like Walker." Toni stuffed her math book into her book bag.

"You have to do homework, right?"

"Yes."

"You have to read books, study hard, and pass tests, right?"

"Sure."

"They can teach me to sing better, right?"

"You're good enough to be the lead singer in the musicals," Toni said.

"Then what's there to be scared of, Toni? Making new friends? You'll be there with me, so I'll have one good friend."

"Maybe I won't, Mattie," Toni said.

"Yes, you will. You have to be," Mattie said. "If you don't go to King with me, then I'll be terrified."

"Really, Mattie Mae Benson?"

"Really, Antoinette Marie Douglas."

Over the weekend, Toni studied, repeating her mantra faithfully morning and night.

Much too soon, the morning of the exam dawned. Buoyed by encouraging hugs and kisses from her parents, Toni waited for Mattie by the mailbox. Even Carl sensed her nervousness, and he gave her five lemon drops from his stash to suck on during the test.

Before Toni entered the school building, Raymond caught her arm. Mattie went on inside.

"This is for you," he said, thrusting a sheet of paper into her hand.

Surprised, Toni shifted her books and unfolded the gift. Across the sheet of white computer paper in large bold black capital letters was "GO TONI!!!" Each letter was made up of small dots.

"You did this on the computer?" she asked.

"No." Then he grinned. "Sure I did. This was an easy program to write. You like it?"

"No," Toni teased, "I love it. Thanks, Raymond. I'll hang it in my room."

"Good. Better get to the test."

The classroom desks had been rearranged into orderly, straight rows. Raymond was sitting right in front of her, and Mattie was to her left. She held the Garfield eraser for good luck.

Mrs. Swallow passed out two sharpened number-two pencils with spanking clean erasers to each student. "Now, class, I hope you all got a good night's sleep, ate your breakfast, and came prepared to do your best," said Mrs. Swallow, her voice enthusiastic. "I'm going to pass out the test. Don't open your test booklets until I tell you to."

Scratch paper was passed out. Toni asked for more. Mrs. Swallow told the class to open the test booklets to page one and read along with her silently as she read the directions aloud. Toni breathed a sigh of relief. The first two subtests were reading vocabulary and reading comprehension, her best subjects.

When her teacher announced the starting time, Toni's heart raced. The adrenaline shot through her veins. She buried her head in the test, completing the first two subtests well before the allotted time was up, allowing her the luxury of going back to check her answers carefully.

The next test was spelling. You had to find the correct spelling from a list of five words, four of which were misspelled. Recalling her inability to do well in spelling bees, Toni doubled her concentration. She sucked on a lemon drop.

"Class, close your test booklet and place your pencil on the right side of your desk."

Toni lowered her head onto her desk, watching Mattie stretch. Loud talk diffused the tension in the room. And when the recess bell rang, the children eagerly fled the room for the open, clean air of the playground. Toni and Mattie walked around, not saying much. The bell rang again too soon.

Toni completed the English usage and map- and graph-reading subtests with ease. Then the class was given a five-minute water and stretch break. This was it! The conceptual, computational, and word problem math tests were next.

Toni fell behind Mattie as they approached the room.

Mrs. Swallow held the door open for her, smiling. Toni couldn't smile back. Mattie gave her a nod of encouragement before she took her seat.

Mrs. Swallow read the directions, asking if anyone had any questions and pausing while the clock ticked on loudly. Then she wrote the time on the board. The first subtest was mathematical concepts. There were forty problems that had to be done in thirty-five minutes!

Oh, no, not even one minute per problem! How can I get them all done? Toni panicked, frantically grabbing for the pencils and scratch paper. Then she forced herself to close her eyes and whisper, "I will use this test to show what I know."

"Ready. Set. Go!" said Mrs. Swallow.

Twenty minutes later, Toni had completed twenty-two of the forty problems. The clock was leaving her behind. When Mrs. Swallow called time and told the children to turn to the next subtest, mathematics computation, she had five problems left to do.

"All right, remember to pace yourselves and estimate your answer. No talking. Raise your hand if you need another pencil or more scratch paper," Mrs. Swallow said. "Ready. Set. Go!"

Toni groaned. This subtest had forty-five problems, and the students were allowed forty minutes to do them. Again, less than one minute per problem. Toni found that if she skipped the ones she knew were trouble and completed the easy ones, she kept her edge. Glancing at the moving hand of the clock, she went back to several that she was unsure of. She sucked on her third lemon drop.

Toni wrestled with each problem until the teacher called time. She was perspiring, and her head was aching from the grinding pressure.

After another short break, the class settled down for the final subtest, mathematics problem solving. There were twenty-nine word problems, each with four answers, only one of which was correct. Toni had forty minutes!

"Now, this is the last test."

The kids cheered. Toni felt eyes on her. Mattie gave her a warm grin and a wink. Raymond turned around and gave her the thumbs-up sign. Mustering her confidence, Toni concentrated on the teacher's last set of instructions.

"Now, remember what I taught all of you about solving word problems because I won't be able to help you now. Any questions?" She passed out more scratch paper. Toni bit her fingernails when an image of Susan crossed her mind.

"No, I can't think about her now. I have to think about scoring high enough to get into King." And it was at that moment that Toni fully realized she wanted to go to King, wanted to make the changes, as scary as they were.

"Ready. Set. Go!" said Mrs. Swallow, writing the starting time and the ending time on the board. Gulping, Toni picked up her pencil and grabbed her scratch paper. She would need to draw pictures of the problems. The first of the twenty-nine problems was about a school class that took a trip to Washington, D.C. She had to calculate the total distance they traveled, including the distance between two different sites, in kilometers. Disobeying her teacher's instructions not to mark in the test booklet, Toni circled and underlined certain information lightly.

This is easy. All I have to do is to add the distances, she thought, quickly arriving at a number. *Tricky. They have one number like mine and one a little larger and another answer that says 'Not Given.'* She added the numbers again and hastily blacked in the correct bubble on the answer sheet.

After taking a couple of long, slow breaths, Toni moved to the next problem. And the next and the next. She repeated her mantra until she reached the nineteenth problem and read:

> Susan has worked as a baby-sitter for several months and saved $78.35. If she spends $69.87 for a new bike, how much money will she have left?

The pencil slipped out of Toni's hand. Surprised, she sat there, seeing the problem and not seeing it. The clock moved forward, and Mrs. Swallow announced twenty more minutes. Toni shook her head. She had to go on.

Skipping that problem, Toni scanned the next one, hurriedly marking the important numbers and figuring out the answer. She continued. When time was called, there were three left to do, plus the one about Susan and her bike. Dejected, Toni passed her test booklet and answer sheet forward.

"How did you do?" Mattie asked.

"I don't know. There were four that I didn't even finish," said Toni. "I don't think I did well enough to get into King unless I got every one of the other twenty-five right, and that would be impossible!"

"I don't think they expect us to be able to finish every problem."

"Did you finish every problem?"

"Yes," Mattie said.

"Why didn't I get your brains?" Toni felt even worse.

When Mrs. Swallow told the class that it would be at least three weeks before she got the results, Toni laid her head on her desk. How could she wait all that time? It seemed like forever.

13

How Much Is Left?

Because her parents both got home late, there were no questions about the test before dinner. But as soon as they were all seated, it began.

"So, how did it go?" asked her father.

"I did real good on all the reading, spelling, and English," Toni said.

"And the math?" Her mother pushed Carl's glass away from his elbow.

"I don't know," Toni said. "I really tried, but some problems I didn't have enough time to get to."

"How long before you get the results?" Her father chewed thoughtfully.

"Mrs. Swallow told us it would be at least three weeks."

"Well, we know you did your best and that's what

counts," said her mother.

Before Toni got into bed she closed her door. On her knees, she prayed, *Dear God, please let me pass the test and get into King. Please don't let me disappoint Daddy and Mama, and me, too. Thank you. Amen. Please bless everyone and take care of Susan. Amen.*

Toni had pinned the banner from Raymond on the wall above her bed. She gazed up, wishing she felt like a GO TONI!!!

Some of the days that followed dragged by. Others ended before Toni realized they had begun. She felt better, knowing that Mattie was anxious. And worse, because if Mattie was worried, then she should be terrified! Raymond was his usual unflappable self.

In the second week after the exam, Toni ran downstairs to ask Mrs. Stamps for help with a shawl she was crocheting for her mother. The yarn was a rich creamy white, part mohair, and difficult to work with. Toni was stuck on the border, a complicated series of puff stitches. The fringe on each end would be the easy part.

"Hi, Mrs. Stamps. Is this a good time?" she asked.

"Fine. I just got home from church and was feeding Hannibal," she said, looking pretty in a pink suit and white silk blouse. "Oh, you've got that beautiful shawl with you. Is that border giving you a fit?"

Toni laughed. "I am going crazy!"

"We'll fix that."

While Mrs. Stamps fed Hannibal, Toni sorted out

her hooks, yarn, and the page of instructions for the border.

"Wasn't it good to see the Lawrences back at church today?" she commented. "I'd missed them. I was afraid they might decide to stay in California."

"Me, too," admitted Toni.

"How are you doing now? About Susan, I mean."

"Better. Last week I went to the phone and started dialing her phone number. But right now what I'm really worried about is the test."

"Did you find out anything yet?"

"Nothing yet." Toni gnawed at her nails.

"Heavens, Toni! If you keep biting these, they're going to bleed." Mrs. Stamps picked up Toni's hands and examined them. "Wait a minute. I'm going to get some ointment."

Toni winced as the ointment went over her thumb. She'd bitten that one down to the quick.

"What if I don't get into King? My parents will hate me and I'll be a failure," confessed Toni. "Mattie will get to go and I'll be left behind."

"All that worry would make me bite my fingernails *and* my toenails, Toni my dear." Mrs. Stamps grinned. "Do I need to look at your feet, too?"

Seeing the teasing smile on Mrs. Stamps's face, Toni shook her head. "No, I don't bite my toenails!"

"Seriously, why do you think your parents would hate you?"

"For months they've made a big deal out of King

and the tests. That's all they talk to me about!"

"Do you want to go there, Toni?"

"At first I didn't, but now I do."

"And if the worst happens and you don't get in this year, can you get in next year?" Mrs. Stamps asked.

"If I scored high the next time, I guess so. But I don't want to wait a year. I want to be an early bird."

"Then I hope things work out. We all love you."

"You love me?" Toni stared at Mrs. Stamps's warm, well-lined face.

"You know I do! Now, let's conquer this shawl and please, Toni my dear, will you try to do something for me?" she asked.

"Sure, what is it?"

"Have a little more faith in yourself, and try not to bite your fingernails," she said, patting Toni's hands.

"I'll try, Mrs. Stamps."

The days went on. On an impulse, in the third week, Toni walked past Susan's house. She hadn't seen it in a while. Carl was home with a cold. She stood outside, glad to see that the drapes were open. Her arms were loaded down with books and the finished shawl that she'd taken to school to show her classmates for another of Mrs. Swallow's activities, "Show and Tell." As she stood there, Mother Dear opened the door.

"Toni, how nice to see you. Come on in." Although she hadn't intended to ring the bell or see the Lawrences, Toni went in.

Everything looked the same. The photographs of

Susan were still up, but the door to her room was shut. Father Lawrence sat in the back, playing dominoes with Mr. Captain, and pots bubbled in the kitchen. But the house was so silent. There were no loud records playing, no telephone chatter, no doors opening.

"Are you hungry?" asked Mother Dear, her eyes listless. She walked across the kitchen. The white in her hair was startling.

"I just wanted to say hello," Toni said, laying the bag with the shawl on the floor.

Mother Dear sat down. "I almost finished cleaning out . . . my granddaughter's room. If there's anything you'd like to have, tell me, Toni."

Susan's beautiful sweaters, minidresses, skirts, the TV, cassette player, jewelry, purses, tapes, and records flashed through Toni's mind.

"Father Lawrence and I are giving most of Susan's belongings to the church," Mother Dear said, her voice falling off. "But if there are things you'd like, it would make us happy to give them to you. You two were good friends. You were a good influence on my granddaughter, Toni. Don't look so surprised. I know she could be a handful. A lot like me when I was young."

Toni hesitated. "There is one thing."

"What is it?"

"The old Raggedy Ann doll, Mother Dear. I don't want anything else." Toni's heart thudded. She was sure it could be heard over the ring of the telephone.

Mother Dear smiled, a long, deep, for-real one.

"That doll is still there. Do you want to get her? I must answer the telephone."

Toni had no choice. She opened the door to Susan's room and tiptoed in. The shades were drawn, filling the room with soft, filtered sunlight. There was the doll. Toni stared at the beds, the closet, the desk. Everything was there but Susan. Holding the doll, she closed the door. Mother Dear was back in the kitchen.

"That was Reverend Webster, calling to see how we were. He's coming for dinner tonight." Mother Dear saw the doll. "Oh, Susan loved that doll. I gave it to her when she was about three. I'm happy that you'll have Annie."

"Has that man gone to jail yet?" Toni asked.

"The verdict came in this morning. He was sentenced to three years." Mother Dear shook her head.

Toni reached for her books and the shawl. The shawl was precious. And so was Mother Dear and all the hours she'd spent in this home, in this kitchen.

"I have to leave now, Mother Dear," she said. "But I want to give you this." Toni lifted the shawl out of the bag and gave it to Susan's grandmother.

"Toni, this is beautiful. But why? You don't have to — "

"I just want to, Mother Dear," Toni said, her voice shaky. And it was true. She did want to leave something of herself there, in Mother Dear's hands.

"Why, thank you, Toni." Tears spilled from Mother Dear's eyes. "Every time I wear this lovely shawl, I'll think of you and the happy times you and Susan shared together."

Toni smiled.

The next day the test results were announced. Mattie had scored highest in the class, except for reading, where Toni had outscored her by one year. Raymond had placed in the top five. Toni examined the slip of paper with her results. All of the reading, spelling, and language scores were three to four grades above grade level. *Where are the math results?* Toni thought. Then she found them! Mathematics concepts, 7.9; mathematics computation, 8.2; and, most important of all, mathematics problem solving, 8.0!

"Mattie, I did it! I did it!" shouted Toni, oblivious to the other kids. "I did it! Do you think my scores are high enough for King?"

"I don't know. Mrs. Swallow said we have to wait to get the letter from King," Mattie said. "But you really pulled those scores up, Toni! Congratulations."

The mailbox in the hallway of her building became the center of Toni's life. Each day she ran home, dropped her books to the floor, and opened the mailbox. Finally a letter came from King Academy. It was addressed to her parents. Toni dared not open it. So she called her parents at work and begged them to come home as early as possible.

They got home at the same time. Before they got their coats off, Toni handed her father the envelope.

He tore it open. "The letter is from The Office of the Principal. Looks like a form letter. Let's see." Then he read the contents aloud:

Dear Mr. and Mrs. Douglas:
I am pleased to inform you that your daughter, Antoinette, has been placed on the waiting list as a beginning seventh-grade student for the fall class. Her scores, when ranked with those of other entering students, placed her in the acceptance group but on the waiting list, due to our limited space. We often have unexpected space in the fall, due to students moving, making other school plans, etc. So I am confident that there will be room for your daughter at King Academy.
However, please check with the main office in August, when we finalize our enrollment figures. Congratulations to you and Antoinette.
Sincerely,
Dr. Marvin Lewis

"What does the letter mean, Daddy?" Toni asked, her eyes wide.

"Just what we wanted. You'll probably get into King." He hugged her. "They have only so much room and a lot of smart applicants like you. We'll know for sure in August."

"I'm so proud of you, honey," her mother said.

"So am I. My CPA exam is coming up, and I am going to pass just the way you did, Pumpkin." Toni's father smiled.

The phone rang.

"Did you get your letter?" Mattie asked.

"Yeah. You?"

"Just now. Toni, what did yours say?"

"I got in but I got placed on the waiting list, so I won't know for sure until August."

Mattie was quiet.

"What about you?" Toni asked.

"I got in. The letter said that I start in September."

"No waiting list?"

"No."

"That's great, Mattie. Look, I have to go now," Toni said.

"Wait a minute, please," Mattie said. "Don't get upset. We're going to King together. I know you'll get in. My mother told me they always have space. She worked there last year as an attendance clerk. If you make the waiting list, you're admitted."

"No fooling, Mattie?"

"Toni Douglas, I'm telling you the truth! We are both going to King in September!"

"Oh, I hope so," Toni said. "I hope there's room for me. Bye, Mattie. See you tomorrow."

Before she could get up, the phone rang again. Raymond called to tell her that he was on the waiting list for King.

Feeling happier, Toni went to wash up. Her father was taking them out to dinner for a family celebration.

Much later that night, too excited to sleep, Toni got

up and sat at her desk. Outside it was chilly. Trees, bearing new growth, swayed in the wind. She sat there a long time, thinking of many things. In her arms she held Annie, the Raggedy Ann doll. And, somewhere beyond the shadows, she listened to the melody of a music box.